IRELAND LORELEI

Sugar and Spice
A Dark Christmas Romance

WARPRESS
PUBLISHING

First edition

This book was professionally typeset on Reedsy.
Find out more at reedsy.com

Contents

Note to Readers

⚜

The characters in this book are unapologetic and dramatic. The scenes are steamy and the road to happily ever after maybe twisted. This book is meant for audiences 18 years old and older. A list of potential triggering themes can be found on my website at https://irelandlorelei.com/possible-triggers

The story within these pages is completely fictional but the concepts of BDSM are real. If you do choose to participate in the BDSM lifestyle, please research it carefully and take all precautions to protect yourself. Fiction is based on real life, but real life is not based on fiction. Remember – Safe, Sane, and Consensual!

If you find any errors, I would like to hear about them. Please screenshot the page and email then to me at ireland@irelandlorelei.com

Please write a review on www.irelandlorelei.com www.warrioresspub and Goodreads. If you would also, write one on Amazon, Kobo, Barnes & Noble or wherever you got your copy that would be greatly appreciated.

Chapter One

Aaliyah Evans

I t is the end of November and Christmas is just around the corner. My parents passed away a few years ago, my father of cancer and my mother a short few months after him. The doctors said of natural causes, but the people of the town said it was due to a broken heart from my dad passing. Now, I don't have any family left. The only thing I have is my bakery, Sugar & Spice.

I grew up here where the snow-capped peaked mountains frame this little town of Ouray, Colorado. We, the locals, like to call it our secret haven, even as the tourist start to flock in more and more as the years pass by. The more the word gets out about our Christmas festivities, the more people that show up to see it.

* * *

As I sit here inside the bakery after closing, I stare out into the night watching the snow fall. It's this time of year that makes me miss my parents so much. My mind starts to flash with memories of growing up like pages of a cherished photo album, each one more vivid than the last.

As I close my eyes and travel back in time, I can vividly recall our cozy family home. It was a charming cottage with a white picket fence, standing proudly against the backdrop of majestic mountains. The garden, lovingly tended by my mother, was a riot of colors in the spring and a tranquil sea of green in the summer. It was where I spent countless hours playing, my small hands covered in dirt as I helped plant flowers under the watchful eye of my mother.

My parents were the anchors of my world. My father, a tall, sturdy man with a heart as big as the Rockies that surrounded our town, was a source of endless wisdom and gentle guidance. He worked at the local hardware store, and every evening, he would return home, his arms full of stories from the townsfolk and tools that held the promise of a new project. I would sit at his feet, listening with rapt attention as he shared his adventures of the day. My mother, on the other hand, was a vision of grace and warmth. With her long, auburn hair and a smile that could melt even the harshest winter frost, she was the embodiment of kindness. She was the heart of our home, the one who taught me to bake my first batch of cookies and instilled in me a love for all things sweet. It was from her that I inherited my passion for baking, and it was in the haven of our kitchen that we spent countless hours crafting delicious creations together.

Our neighbors were more than just people who lived next door; they were an extension of our family. The Johnson's, the Millers, and the Carters, families with children my age, became lifelong friends. Our summers were filled with bike rides along winding trails, picnics in the meadow, and impromptu games of hide and seek.

The heart of the town, however, was our local community center. Every Friday evening, the town would gather there for a potluck dinner, and the laughter of children and adults alike would echo through the halls. These were the moments that defined the essence of Ouray. We are a tight-knit community that celebrated togetherness and embraced everyone, young and old.

In the winter, when the town was blanketed in a pristine coat of snow, my father would take me sledding down the hills, and my mother would prepare hot cocoa for us to enjoy by the fireplace. Those were the moments when I felt the warmth of our family's love most intensely. The annual Ouray Winter Festival was another cherished tradition. The entire town would gather to watch the majestic ice sculptures, created with meticulous care and artistic precision. I can still feel the crisp winter air on my cheeks as I marveled at the glistening sculptures that seemed to capture the very essence of our town.

In the evenings, we would sit by the fire, and my parents would share stories of their youth, of their dreams and aspirations. It was in those moments that I learned the value of dreams, and they encouraged me to reach for the stars, to follow my passion with unwavering determination. As I reflect on those days, I realize that Ouray was not just a town; it was a cocoon of love, nurturing me and shaping me into the person I am today. My parents, with their unwavering support and boundless love, instilled in me a sense of purpose and the belief that life is a beautiful journey worth savoring.

Oh, how I miss those days. I miss my parents the most. I am

lucky to have the support and love from my friends and the community, but I do get lonely. Love, let's not even think about relationships right now. Those have not been kind to me. It is really hard to find love in a place where you know everyone and you are all so close. I have had a few failed relationships through the years. People move into our quaint little town, but once they decide it is too quiet for them, they leave and this one in particular shattered my heart into a thousand pieces when he left.

* * *

Sugar & Spice is where my heart resides now. I spend every waking moment working in the bakery. I am very proud to be the owner of this picturesque bakery tucked away amidst the breathtaking snow-covered landscape. From the time I was a little girl sitting in my grandmother's kitchen watching as she baked cookies, cakes, fudge and all kinds of goodies for Christmas Day, I knew that I wanted to be a baker and have my own store. It was a dream that after finishing high school I went to the local college and took business classes so I would know how to create and maintain the business and culinary classes to become the best baker I could be, never forgetting my grandmother's recipes that still sit on the menu and in the display cases as special items.

My parents helped me start the bakery after college. They went to the bank and helped me get a loan and assisted in getting all my permits and licenses and all the furniture, etc that I needed to get the bakery up and running.

When you step through the charming, frost-kissed door the aroma of freshly baked pastries and the warmth of a crackling fireplace envelop you like a comforting embrace. It's not just a bakery; it's an experience, a sanctuary of sweetness in the heart of the mountains. This place, my haven, is where dreams are crafted from flour and sugar, and where people find solace in the simplicity of freshly baked treats. It's a piece of my heart, a testament to my love for all things sugary, and a reflection of the joy that comes from sharing that love with others.

The old wooden shelves, polished with love, display an array of delicacies. Rows of cupcakes, each a miniature masterpiece, beckon with their vibrant frosting and intricate designs. The pies, fresh from the oven, send tendrils of cinnamon and apple through the air. Flaky croissants, soft as a winter morning's kiss, grace the display alongside buttery scones adorned with clotted cream. And, of course, the centerpiece, my signature double chocolate layer cake, its velvety layers waiting to melt in the mouths of those who dare to indulge.

Every day the air is filled with the gentle hums of conversations, punctuated by delighted sighs as customers savor the delectable offerings. Friends and strangers gather here, drawn by the promise of something extraordinary, something that transcends the mundane. I greet each customer with a genuine smile, my apron dusted with a touch of flour. The atmosphere is a blend of coziness and enchantment, where the golden light from the chandelier's dances on polished wood, casting intricate shadows on the walls adorned with vintage photographs.

My hands, weathered from years of crafting sugary delights, work with precision and love. Baking is not just my livelihood; it's an art, a passion. Each cupcake I frost, each pie I fill, is a part of me, a testament to the dedication that goes into each creation. I love seeing the delight in the eyes of those who take their first bite, the moment of pure bliss when a sugar-dusted donut touches their lips, and the shared laughter that fills the room as friends gather to enjoy a warm cup of cocoa and a freshly baked cinnamon roll.

Sugar & Spice is not just a bakery; it's a reflection of my life, my dreams, and my connection to this town. It's a place where love and laughter mix with flour and sugar to create memories. It's here, amidst these snowy peaks, that I've found my purpose, and every day, I'm reminded that life is a beautiful blend of sugar and spice.

Chapter Two

Madden Griffin

Today everything changed. I was in the heart of the concrete jungle walking down the street in Manhattan heading to my law office. It was my life now and a world away from the tranquil haven of Ouray, Colorado, where I'd grown up.

My cell phone rang. I answer and the voice on the other end of the line was shaken, choked with emotion, and in an instant, my world unravels.

It is my mom, and her words punched me in the gut, "Madden, your father… he's had a massive heart attack, and… he didn't make it."

I could hardly process the words, my mind a blur of disbelief, shock, and sorrow. My dad, the unshakable force in our family, the man who had always been my rock, was gone. It was as if someone had extinguished the guiding light of my life.

Finally, able to speak, "Mom, calm down. I am on my way. I

will book the first flight home."

I continue into the building and to my office, I shut the door and sit behind my desk. I put my head down in my hands. A knock on the door brings me back from my thoughts, my grief and my tears.

"Mr. Griffin, are you okay?" Sherry, my administrative assistant asks as she opens the door.

I lift my head and say, "Sherry, no I am not okay. I need to go home."

"Are you sick?" Sherry asks.

"No, no. I ummm. My father just died, and I need to go home. Home to Ouray, Colorado. Can you book me on the first flight out, please?" I ask.

"Of course, Sir," Sherry says as she starts to head back out the door, but turns first and says, "I am so sorry for your loss. I will cancel all of your appointments and get with Paul to take on your cases while you are gone."

I couldn't even reply. I just sit here for another minute trying to gather my thoughts. Then I get up and pick up my briefcase and head out of my office. When I walk pass Sherry's desk I tell her, "Call me with the information for the flight when you have it and also email it to me. I am going home to back."

"Yes, Sir," Sherry replies as the elevator door closes.

After I finished packing, my phone pinged with a text from Sherry saying my itinerary is in the email. I rush to the airport through the bustling streets of New York, where I'd built my life as a successful attorney, seemed surreal, a world away from the serene mountains and cozy warmth of home. I sat in the plane, my thoughts in turmoil, battling the realization that I was heading home not for a joyful reunion, but to face the gaping hole that my father's absence had created.

When I land in Ouray, the crisp mountain air and the scent of pine trees enveloped me as I step out of the airport. A bittersweet reminder of the countless childhood memories I'd shared with my father. As I drive the rental car to our family home it is filled with an eerie silence, one that echos the grief that has settles over our town.

I pull the car up to my parents' house and my mom, a picture of strength despite the grief etched on her face, greets me at the door with a tearful embrace. In that moment, I realize the weight she carries, not just as a widow, but as the woman who had stood by my father's side, helping him manage the family ski resort for all these years. The weight of an entire legacy now resting on her shoulders.

After spending the next hour talking about what happened and me holding my mom as she cried, and we shared memories of my dad. My uncle, my dad's brother and his family showed up right after I got here. Then my mom's sister and her son, who was my best friend growing up until they moved away to Detroit because my uncle had gotten a job there when Josh and I were ten, got here just in time to head to the funeral home with us. My mom's brother and brother-in-law had both passed away a few years ago. There really wasn't much family left.

We got to the funeral home and spent hours planning the funeral, every detail a poignant reminder of the man we had lost. The service would be in two days.

* * *

I spent the next two days, just around the house with my family. We shut down the ski resort for the week, so I didn't have to deal with that right now. I didn't go out into town, and I didn't want to be around all the people that showed up to give their condolences so I would stay outback or upstairs. I told mom that I just couldn't see all these people that I barely remembered, tell me how sorry they were, not yet.

The church, where my father had sung in the choir, was filled with the mournful strains of hymns. The eulogies painted a vivid picture of his life, of the countless people he'd touched as the heart and soul of our town. As we stood by his casket, surrounded by friends, family, and well-wishers, the snow began to fall, soft as feathers, a serene reminder of the beauty that had always been a part of my father's world. The day was a blur of condolences and arrangements.

The day after the funeral left me with the weight of the family legacy and the fact that it was now inescapable, a duty I had never wished to bear. My dreams had led me to New York, to a career as a powerful attorney, far removed from the world of ski resorts and snowy slopes. Yet, I couldn't ignore the sense of duty that tugged at my heart. My mother needed me, not just as her son, but as a partner in the monumental task of running the ski resort that had been in our family for generations. The thought of leaving behind my career, the power and prestige I'd earned, was a painful one. But my father's legacy, our legacy, was a promise I couldn't break. In the end, my decision was made not out of obligation, but out of love for my family, for the town of Ouray that had given me so much, and for the memory of my father. I knew the path ahead would be challenging, a journey into uncharted territory, but it was a journey I would undertake with unwavering determination. Returning to Ouray, I came home not just to honor my father's memory, but to embrace a new chapter in my life, one that would see me taking the reins of the ski resort, a daunting task that would test the mettle of the man I had become in my years away from home.

As I walked through the familiar streets of Ouray, I couldn't help but wonder how this homecoming would reshape the trajectory of my life, a life I had once thought was set in stone but was now a blank page awaiting a new story, a story that would honor the legacy of my father, the man who had been my greatest inspiration.

The smells of baked goods was radiating down the street. I followed it to this little bakery called Sugar and Spice. As soon as I opened the door, my stomach started to growl. I walked up to the counter to look inside the glass counters and that's when I saw her. Her back was turned to me, but man she had a body that was out of this world. She was in a pair of jeans and a pink t-shirt that read "Sugar & Spice" on it. Her blond hair hung down her back and her skin was the beautiful color of caramel. When she turned around, she smiled at me, and that smile was one that I had never forgotten; Aaliyah Evans…damn…what a sight!

Chapter Three

❦

Aaliyah

In the soft, early morning light, I stand in the heart of my bakery, surrounded by the intoxicating aroma of freshly baked pastries. The rhythmic sound of my stand mixer fills the room, an old friend that has seen me through countless hours of baking, contemplation, and healing. This bakery is not just a place of confections; it's a sanctuary, a cocoon where my heart has found solace, a haven where I've retreated from the tumultuous tides of love.

My hands, accustomed to the gentle artistry of baking, move with precision as I carefully measure out ingredients. Flour, sugar, and butter – these are the constants in my life, the ingredients that never disappoint, never leave me yearning for more. The buttery dough beneath my fingers is soft and malleable, a blank canvas awaiting my touch, much like the pages of my life, waiting to be written upon once more. With each measured scoop of flour, my mind wanders down the labyrinthine path of my past, a trail lined with love and heartbreak, each turn a new chapter in a story that has shaped me. I've loved and lost, been swept off my feet and left on shaky ground. It's as if the universe has been orchestrating a series of lessons, teaching me that love is a beautiful but perilous dance.

There was Steven, my high school sweetheart, with his warm smile and the promise of forever. We used to sneak out on warm summer nights, our fingers entwined as we explored the starlit world. But forever didn't last, and like the fireflies we'd chase, our love flickered and faded, leaving me with a bittersweet memory. But who actually believes that a high school love lasts. Boys in high school have no idea what love really means. They really do mature slower than girls. It took me years though to really figure that out and even then, it still hurt the same.

Then there was Troy, my college love, the one who taught me that love can be fluid, transcending boundaries and expectations. He showed me a world of love that was beautifully complex and wonderfully free, yet even in that love, there were lessons to learn, boundaries to navigate. Then he dumped me without any explanations and wouldn't take my calls or my text messages. I was devastated and didn't think I would ever open up my heart again. And then I met Alex.

Alex was the passionate writer with a heart full of stories. We'd spend hours in coffee shops, discussing characters and plot twists, our connection as deep as the plots we crafted. But much like the characters in our stories, our relationship took unexpected turns, leading to an ending I couldn't have foreseen. We had met at a diner in the town over one evening. I was sitting alone and so was he. He was at the table beside me. He asked if he could join me and well that started a whole relationship until six months later, I found out he was married.

The memories of Alex still linger in my mind, like a bittersweet ghost of love lost. Alex was the passionate writer, a man whose heart was overflowing with stories and ideas, much like the pages of a book he had yet to write. Our connection had been a tapestry of shared dreams, interwoven with discussions of characters and plot twists that came alive in the coffee shops where we'd spend hours. I remember the day we first met at that diner in the town over, a chance encounter that would set the course of our relationship. I had been sitting alone, sipping my coffee, when he approached. The invitation to join me was polite and unassuming, and in that moment, I couldn't have known how it would change the trajectory of my life. We talked about everything and nothing, the conversation flowing as naturally as a river's current. I was drawn to his intellect, his passion for storytelling, and the way he seemed to see the world through a unique lens. It was as if we were co-authors of our own story, crafting characters and narratives that danced across the canvas of our lives. In those first few months, it felt like we were living in a storybook romance. We explored the town, its hidden gems and secret spots, making memories that would stay with me forever. It was a whirlwind of emotion, passion, and adventure. I opened my heart to him, trusting him with my deepest hopes and fears, just as he did with me. But then, like the unexpected plot twists we used to create in our stories, our relationship took a turn I couldn't have foreseen. It was six months into our love story when I discovered the truth. He was married. The realization was a gut-wrenching blow, a revelation that shattered the fairy tale we had been living. I still remember the day I found out, the way my heart sank as I uncovered the painful secret. The weight of his betrayal was crushing, the disbelief and heartbreak leaving me in a state of shock.

It was one cold night, and we were sitting at the diner where we had met as the woman confronted Alex, her voice trembling with a mix of hurt and anger, the entire diner seemed to hold its breath. Conversations hushed, and the clinking of cutlery against plates ceased. All eyes were on our table, and I felt like a trapped animal, caught in a spotlight.

"Alex," she continued, her voice louder, her frustration evident, "you can't keep doing this. We need to talk about our marriage."

My heart pounded in my chest, and I realized that I had been living a lie, a lie constructed by the man who had sat across from me, professing his love. But the truth was undeniable, standing right there before me. In that charged moment, Alex struggled to find words, his gaze darting between the woman and me. The tension was suffocating, and I had to say something, to break the silence that threatened to consume us.

"Who are you?" I finally managed to ask with a shaky voice. It was a question born of desperation, a plea for clarity in a situation that was spiraling out of control.

The woman turned her gaze to me, and for the first time, her eyes met mine. They were filled with a mixture of sadness and understanding. "I'm Alex's wife," she replied, her words heavy with the weight of the truth.

The admission hung in the air, like a damning verdict. The realization that I had been the other woman, unknowingly entangled in a web of deceit, washed over me in a wave of humiliation and pain. The diner, once a place of comfort and familiarity, had transformed into a battlefield of emotions. Tears welled up in my eyes as the truth sank in. I had been betrayed, and the pain was inescapable. The woman's voice quivered as she continued to speak, recounting their history, their marriage, and the pain she had endured. Her words were a painful testament to the reality of the situation. As she spoke, her emotions grew more intense, and her voice carried through the diner, her words like a piercing lament. A scene was unfolding, a public confrontation that left me feeling exposed and vulnerable. I couldn't bear to remain in that place any longer, surrounded by the prying eyes and the painful truth. With tears streaming down my cheeks, I rose from my seat and hurried toward the exit, the sound of the woman's voice echoing in my ears. The world outside was a blur as I stepped into the cool night, the shock and heartbreak of the revelation still fresh and raw.

The pain of that discovery, the feeling of being deceived and betrayed, was etched into my heart. It was a wound that ran deep, one that took a long time to heal. I made a promise to myself that day, a solemn vow that I would never look for love again. I couldn't bear the thought of opening my heart only to be hurt once more. That promise became my shield, my fortress of protection. I threw myself into my bakery, finding solace in the creation of sweet delights. Love had wounded me, and I vowed never to let it happen again. As I sit in my bakery now, reminiscing about Alex and the painful lesson he taught me, I can't help but feel a sense of gratitude for the haven I've created for myself.

And these three were just the three longest of my relationships and the most hurtful, there were many other heartbreaks through the years. Each of these relationships had carved their marks on my heart, and with every heartbreak, I retreated deeper into the welcoming embrace of my bakery. It was here that I discovered solace in the simplicity of baking, a refuge from the tumultuous world of love. In the delicate folds of pastry and the swirls of frosting, I found a sense of control, a way to channel my emotions and create something beautiful.

But it's more than just heartbreak that has led me to this place. It's a choice, a conscious decision to focus on myself, to build a life that's truly my own. I've seen how love can be both an intoxicating elixir and a dangerous poison. It left me adrift searching for solid ground. It is that journey that has brought me here, where I've poured my heart into crafting exquisite creations, where I've sought solace and comfort in the midst of flour and sugar.

As the golden morning light streams through the windows, I can't help but smile as I take in the array of pastries, each one a testament to my journey, my resilience, and my love for the art of baking. This bakery is a reflection of my life, my dreams, and my connection to this town. It's a place where love and laughter mix with flour and sugar to create memories.

Chapter Four

Aaliyah

I'm in the middle of a perfectly executed raspberry-filled donut, the kind that oozes with sweetness with every bite, when a peculiar sensation washes over me. An inexplicable pull makes me turn around, and there he is, standing near the entrance of my bakery. Madden Griffin, or as I remember him from our high school days, Mr. Tall, Dark, and Handsome. He was the senior homecoming king, the basketball star who could charm his way through any crowd, and now, here he was, back in Ouray. I had heard that he had come home about a week ago after his father passed for the funeral. I had heard a few rumors that he might stay longer to help his mom with the family business. I also heard he was moving back in order to take over the family business. But I won't ask him. I know that whatever is really going on with him, it has to be a tough decision. One thing I do know is that he will be the dutiful son he's always been. I admire his devotion, his sense of duty, even as I wonder how the bustling streets of New York have molded the boy I used to know.

Our eyes meet, and for a moment, I feel like time has folded in on itself. It's been years since I've seen him, and while he's undoubtedly matured, there's still that familiar twinkle in his eyes. The same eyes that used to watch me from the basketball court as I cheered for my beloved team. His gaze lingers, and in that instant, I'm taken back to those carefree days of high school, when anything felt possible.

I can't help but offer a warm smile, our past intertwined in those brief glances. The small town of Ouray has a way of bringing people back together, even if just for a moment. "Madden?" I say, feeling a touch of disbelief in my own voice.

He grins, and the familiarity in his face is both comforting and unsettling. "Aaliyah," he replies, his voice carrying the same charisma I remember. "It's been a long time."

As we stand at the counter chatting, exchanging pleasantries and the usual 'how have you been?' questions, my employee, Rene, a high school senior, bursts in for her afternoon shift. Rene walks around to stand beside me behind the counter. I introduce her to Madden, and she looks at us both and then says, "Aaliyah I can handle everything. You two go ahead and grab a table and get caught up."

I shake my head and walk around the counter, and we head to a table by the window. Madden pulls out my chair for me and I sit down. As we start conversing, we sip our cups of coffee and share stories about high school, our classes, and our shared memories of a town that holds a special place in all our hearts. I can't help but feel a twinge of nostalgia as I listen, reminiscing about the time when I was just a sophomore cheerleader and Madden was a senior on the basketball team, guiding our team to victory.

In his presence, I can see the same charisma that made him a beloved figure in high school. It's almost surreal, the way our past and present have collided in my bakery, a place that has always been my sanctuary, my refuge.

As we continue our conversation, I'm struck by the contrast between the past and the present. We are all grown up, evolved, and have taken different life paths. I, with my bakery and the comfort I've found in creating delightful pastries, and Madden, with a successful life in the legal world, far removed from the snow-covered mountains of Ouray.

Despite the years that have passed, this unexpected reunion with Madden feels like a bridge connecting our past to the present. Memories flood my mind, a whirlwind of emotions that I hadn't anticipated. Madden was the boy that every girl dreamed about, even myself, though I had never dared to admit it. He was the epitome of charm and popularity, a senior who had effortlessly captured the essence of our small-town high school life. I was a cheerleader, yes, but I was also two years younger than him, and in my eyes, light-years away from the world he inhabited. I had watched him from the sidelines, a quiet observer of his life. Madden was the homecoming king, the basketball star, and the guy who seemed to have it all. He was the one the girls gushed about, the one whose name echoed through the hallways as if he were a legend. But in my quieter moments, I knew my place in the grand tapestry of our high school hierarchy. I wasn't the girl that someone as gorgeous and popular as Madden would look at twice, much less consider dating. It wasn't a matter of self-pity, but rather a quiet acknowledgment of the social realities that shaped our world. It was the unspoken understanding that some people, like Madden, existed on a different plane, untouched by the insecurities that plagued the rest of us. I never allowed myself to harbor illusions of being noticed by someone like him, not when there were prettier, smarter, and more confident girls to catch his attention. I was content to cheer from the bleachers, my heart quietly yearning for the boy who had no idea I even existed. It was a dream, a secret fantasy that I kept hidden in the depths of my heart, a world where a girl like me could be seen as more than just a shadow on the periphery of his life.

As the seasons passed, we each ventured into our own worlds. Madden, the star athlete, pursued his education and career, while I, the quiet observer, sought solace in my books and the art of baking. Our paths had diverged, and I had long accepted that I was destined for a different life, one where love and relationships were distant stars in a vast, unreachable sky.

Now, in this moment, as we reconnect in my bakery, I'm faced with the boy who had always been just a dream. The boy who had no idea that, beneath the facade of the sophomore cheerleader, there had been a heart that yearned for something more, something that felt like the elusive magic of high school romance. The years have changed us both, molded us into the adults we've become. Yet, as we sit together, sharing stories of our past, I can't help but wonder if this unexpected reunion is more than just a chance encounter. Perhaps it's a reminder that life has a way of weaving its own narratives, stories that transcend the boundaries we once believed were set in stone.

Madden's presence brings a strange mix of nostalgia and curiosity. The girl who once believed she was unworthy of his attention now finds herself wondering about the chapters that are yet to be written. The cheerleader who once watched from the sidelines is now a woman who has discovered her own strength, her own identity. As I look into Madden's eyes, I'm aware that time has a way of erasing the boundaries of the past, allowing for new connections and possibilities. The boy who was once the embodiment of a dream is now a man sitting before me, and the future remains an open book, waiting to be filled with stories that neither of us could have predicted.

Chapter Five

Madden

I find myself sitting in the stillness of my parent's kitchen. The place where I grew up and where I remember having thoughts about Aaliyah in high school. My thoughts are still lingering on the unexpected encounter at the bakery. Aaliyah, the name brings back a flood of memories, of basketball games and high school dances, of a time when I was young and carefree. Seeing her again after so many years, I couldn't help but feel a rush of emotions that caught me off guard.

In high school, Aaliyah was the kind of girl that everyone noticed, including me, even though I was the homecoming king and one of the popular kids. It was the way she carried herself, the grace and charm that set her apart from the rest. She was two years younger, a sophomore cheerleader with a smile that could light up any room. From my vantage point as a senior on the basketball team. I was focused on my future, but I couldn't help but have a crush on her. It was clear that she was something special. There was something about

25

her that drew me in, a certain grace and charm that transcended the typical high school dynamics.

It's funny how the world of high school operates. I was surrounded by girls who threw themselves at me, their attention and affection so palpable that it was impossible to ignore. Yet, amidst all that clamor, there was one girl who had always remained elusive, Aaliyah. She was the exception, the enigma that defied the conventions of our teenage world.

I remember her vividly, cheering from the sidelines at our basketball games. Her presence on the bleachers was like a beacon of light, and as I would glance in her direction, I couldn't help but feel a rush of nervous excitement. She was the girl who had always been just out of reach, a fleeting presence in my teenage dreams. She was different from the girls who clamored for my attention. She didn't vie for the spotlight or the chance to be noticed. Instead, she was content to shine in her own quiet way, a graceful figure on the edges of my high school world. It was the way she carried herself, the confidence that came from within, that drew me in.

I couldn't help but be drawn to her, despite the adulation and admiration I received from others. She was a mystery, an uncharted territory that I had never dared to explore. I was the popular kid, the homecoming king, the one who had it all, and yet, she remained the one who intrigued me. There was an authenticity to Aaliyah, a genuineness that set her apart. While the other girls seemed to be trying so hard to fit into a mold, she remained true to herself. It was as if she had unlocked the secret to being comfortable in her own skin, a quality that was both rare and captivating. And so, my crush on her had grown silently, like a bud on the verge of blooming. I would find myself stealing glances in her direction during those basketball games, hoping for a moment of eye contact, a shared smile that would bridge the gap between us. But it had always felt like an impossible *dream, one that I never had the courage to pursue.*

The truth was, I never believed someone like Aaliyah would be interested in someone like me. She was smart, kind, and incredibly beautiful, while I was just the senior who happened to be good at basketball. It was as if the boundaries of our high school social hierarchy were etched in stone, and she existed on a different plane, one that was far beyond my reach. She was the girl who didn't conform to the superficiality of high school dynamics, and I admired her for it. But that admiration was tinged with the understanding that she deserved better than the typical high school romance, better than a guy like me who couldn't find the words to bridge the divide.

As the years have passed and we find ourselves sitting in her bakery, sharing stories and rediscovering our connection, I can't help but reflect on the teenage dreams and the boundaries that once held us back. It's a reminder that life has a way of weaving its own narratives, sometimes in unexpected and surprising ways. Aaliyah, the girl who was once just a dream, is now a woman who has crafted her own path, a path that has led her to this very moment.

Our encounter at the bakery was a blast from the past, and yet, there was something different about her. She had grown into a confident and poised woman, a far cry from the young girl I used to know. I couldn't help but be captivated by her presence, her easy confidence, and the smile that still had the power to take my breath away.

As the evening unfolded, we had talked about our lives since high school. She told me about her bakery, her passion for baking, and the refuge it had become for her. I couldn't help but admire her dedication and the strength she exuded. It was clear that she had carved out a life for herself, one that was separate from the high school world we had once known.

Even today as we sat there, a flood of not just memories hit me like a ton of bricks, but also the feelings of being given a second chance to tell the girl that I let get away how I felt about her all those years ago. The thing that really took me off guard was that all those feelings came flooding back and now they felt different than they were before. They feel more powerful. I assume it is because we have grown not just in age, but in maturity and she had definitely filled out more. I couldn't help but watch her ass swish back and forth and she walked around the counter in front of me to a table today, or the way her breasts looked in that shirt.

* * *

The next day, I found myself at the ski resort, the place that had been a cornerstone of my life for as long as I could remember. As a young boy, I had followed my father and grandfather around, learning the business from the ground up. I remembered the thrill of the slopes, the taste of freshly fallen snow, and the satisfaction of a hard day's work in the crisp mountain air.

The scenery around the resort was as breathtaking as ever. The slopes glistened with fresh snow, the mountains stood tall and proud, and the crispness of the air invigorated me. The main building was bustling with activity, skiers and snowboarders gearing up for a day on the slopes, laughter and excitement filling the air.

I made my way to my father's office, a room that had always held a certain mystique for me. It was here that he had made decisions that shaped the course of our family business, a business that had been passed down through generations. I couldn't help but feel a sense of loss as I sat at his desk, his absence a palpable presence in the room.

My memories of this place were intertwined with my father's guidance, his patient teachings, and the dreams he had instilled in me. I had left this world behind to pursue a career as an attorney in New York, a path that had brought me success and power. But now, returning to my roots, I was faced with the reality of running the ski resort, a responsibility I had never imagined shouldering. The weight of my father's passing bore down on me, the realization that I was now the one to carry forward the legacy of our family. It was a daunting task, one that I had no choice but to embrace. As I looked out the window, the view of the slopes and the bustling activity of the ski shop, I knew that there was no turning back.

The decision to call my law firm in New York and inform them of my resignation weighed heavily on my mind. I had built a successful career, earned the respect of my peers, and carved out a niche in a competitive world. But my sense of duty to my family and to the ski resort was unwavering. I decided to wait until my leave was almost over before making that call, a choice that was both strategic and difficult. The days ahead were going to be filled with challenges and uncertainties, and I couldn't help but wonder how this abrupt shift in my life's trajectory would shape my future.

As I continued to sit there with the memories of my past mingling with the weight of my new responsibilities, I knew that my return to Ouray was more than just a visit. It was a reconnection with my roots, a rekindling of old friendships, and a new chapter in my life that was about to unfold.

Chapter Six

Madden

The moment has come to reopen the ski resort. I stand at the precipice of a new beginning, one that's tinged with uncertainty and a since of obligation instead of excitement. The weight of this responsibility is undeniable, and as I prepare to step into this new future that my life has been given, a future that I didn't want to face, I can't help but feel mixed emotions. The manager of the resort was already there when I called this morning. Mom had told me that he had been efficiently running things for years. It's a testament to his dedication and skill, and it eases the burden of my new responsibilities.

Before I head to the resort, a thought nags at me, Aaliyah. It's been two days since I ran into Aaliyah at the bakery for the first time since I left for college all those years ago. I had promised to return to the bakery and come see her. I have a little time to burn before I head to the resort, and so, I make a detour, deciding to stop in before I take on the day's tasks. As I enter the bakery, the rich aroma of freshly baked pastries envelops me, a comforting reminder of the warmth within these walls. I decide to take a seat at a corner table.

Aaliyah, ever the gracious host, notices my presence and approaches with a warm smile. "Madden, it's good to see you again," she says, and I can't help but feel a sense of ease in her presence.

I return her smile. "Likewise, Aaliyah. How's everything going here?"

As we sit together in the warmth of Aaliyah's bakery, our conversation takes on a more practical tone. We engage in small talk, discussing the reopening of the resort and the challenges that lie ahead.

I lean in, my gaze meeting Aaliyah's as I speak, "So, Aaliyah, I've got quite a task ahead with the resort. Reopening it in such a short time is a bit overwhelming, to be honest."

Aaliyah nods in understanding, her eyes reflecting a mixture of empathy and concern. "I can only imagine the work that needs to be done. It's a lot to take on, especially with your background in law."

I appreciate her understanding and reply, "You're right. It's a far cry from the courtroom, but it's a responsibility I can't just walk away from. My mom needs the help, and the resort has been in our family for generations."

Aaliyah leans forward, her expression thoughtful. "Family businesses are important. I can see why you'd step in. But it must be a big adjustment."

I smile wryly, "You have no idea. It's been a whirlwind since I got that call about my dad. And I haven't even officially told my law firm in New York that I'm quitting."

Aaliyah's eyes widen in surprise, "You haven't told them yet? That's a major decision."

I sigh, running a hand through my hair. "I know, but I wanted to make sure I can handle this first. The firm will understand, I hope. But it's not an easy call to make."

We continue to discuss the practicalities of the resort's reopening, sharing insights and concerns. Despite the challenges, I'm finding myself strangely grateful for the unexpected support and connection I've found in Aaliyah, a familiar face from my past who has now become a source of understanding and encouragement.

As we continue our conversation in the cozy ambiance of her bakery, the topic naturally shifts back to our high school days, and she begins to share memories. She laughs as she recounts a particularly embarrassing moment from her cheerleading days. Her laughter is infectious, and it's impossible not to be drawn into the stories she weaves.

She leans forward, her eyes dancing with mirth as she recalls, "You won't believe it, but there was this one time during a game, I got tangled in the cheerleader pom-poms, and I couldn't get myself untangled. I must have looked like a total klutz."

I can't help but join in her laughter. It's a genuine, carefree moment, and it feels like a burst of sunshine in the midst of my otherwise heavy responsibilities. "I remember that" I say with a chuckle, my voice tinged with nostalgia. "But you know what, Aaliyah? You always managed to turn things around with your grace and charm."

She looks at me, her eyes sparkling with a mixture of surprise and appreciation. "You remember that?"

I nod, my own memories coming to life. "How could I forget? It was moments like those that made high school more fun."

and I can't help but chuckle.

Our conversation is easy, as if the years apart have had no effect on our connection. She shares stories about her journey, her dreams of owning a bakery, and the hard work she's put into making it a reality. I find myself admiring her even more, not just for her strength but for her ability to follow her passion.

As we sip on coffee and savor danishes, the world outside the bakery seems to disappear. It's just the two of us, and for a moment, I can't help but think about how I'd love to get to know the adult Aaliyah better. The girl I knew from high school has transformed into a remarkable woman, and the curiosity about the path she's taken is impossible to ignore.

The clock ticks, and I realize it's time for me to leave. The resort awaits, along with a plethora of tasks and responsibilities. As I bid Aaliyah farewell, a sense of reluctance washes over me. I can't help but think about her, about the connection we're rekindling, and the desire to see where it might lead.

As I step out of the bakery and head toward the resort, my thoughts are consumed by Aaliyah. The memories of our high school days, the laughter we shared, and the connection we've reestablished play like a movie in my mind. The prospect of reopening the ski resort, with all its challenges, is daunting.

* * *

Leaving Aaliyah's bakery with a sense of gratitude for the warmth and nostalgia our conversation had brought, I made my way to the ski resort. The day had arrived, and it was time to reopen the place that had been in my family for generations. The weight of my responsibilities felt heavy on my shoulders, but there was also a spark of determination within me.

As I walked into the resort, the familiar surroundings triggered a rush of memories. The slopes, the main building, the ski shop, it all felt like a part of me. I had spent my childhood following my father and grandfather around here, learning the ins and outs of the business. It was a world that had always been in the background, a path I never intended to follow until now.

The ski resort was quiet. It was still somewhat early in the morning, the air crisp and invigorating. The manager, a seasoned employee who had been with us for years, was already at work, overseeing the preparations. He looked up as I entered, his face a mix of relief and apprehension.

"Good morning, Mr. Griffin," he greeted me, his voice tinged with respect. "We've been working hard to get everything ready for the reopening."

I nodded, appreciating his dedication. "Thank you, Paul. I know this is a lot to take on in such a short time."

He smiled, a reassuring gesture. "We'll manage, Mr. Griffin. We're a team, and we're here to support you."

As the day went on, we went through the final preparations, checking safety equipment, making sure the slopes were groomed, and ensuring that everything was in order. The staff, many of whom I had known since I was a child, were working diligently, and their loyalty to the resort was evident.

The day of the reopening was filled with its own challenges and setbacks. Some unexpected issues cropped up, but they were dealt with swiftly. It was a day of hard work, but it was also a day of seeing the resort come back to life, a realization that was both rewarding and daunting.

By the time the resort closed for the day, and the last skiers and snowboarders left, I stood there, looking out at the slopes that had once been my playground. The day had been exhausting, and I was bone-tired, but there was also a sense of fulfillment that filled me.

I found Paul and we exchanged a tired but satisfied glance. "We did it," he said with a hint of pride in his voice.

I nodded, the weight on my shoulders feeling a little lighter. "We did. It's going to be a lot of hard work, but I think we can make this place thrive again."

As the resort sat in the tranquil dusk, I couldn't help but reflect on the decision I had made to leave my law career and take over this business. It was a path I had never planned for, and yet, there was a sense of rightness in it. I felt the weight of that responsibility, but I also felt a flicker of hope. This place had been a backdrop to my childhood, a source of cherished memories, and now, it was a challenge I was willing to embrace.

As I locked up and walked away, the stars shining above, I couldn't help but feel a sense of satisfaction, knowing that this was where I was meant to be, carrying on a tradition that had been in my family for generations, a legacy that was now in my hands.

Chapter Seven

Aaliyah

It is three weeks before Christmas and I'm immersed in the whirlwind of holiday preparations. Our little picturesque town is undergoing its annual transformation, dressed in the festive colors of the season. With twinkling lights adorning the streets and the scent of pine and cinnamon in the air, it's impossible not to be swept up in the holiday spirit.

On this particular Friday, as I'm bustling around my bakery, the door chimes, announcing a visitor. I turn, expecting to see a customer, but to my pleasant surprise, it's Madden. His presence is a welcome interruption to my busy day.

He steps into the bakery, a warm smile on his face. "Aaliyah," he greets me. "I hope I'm not interrupting."

I wipe my hands on my apron, genuinely pleased to see him. "Madden," I greet him, genuinely happy to see a familiar face. "You're not interrupting at all. It's always good to have a friend stop by."

He chuckles softly, a sound that fills the bakery with warmth. "I'm glad to hear that. I hope your day is going well."

I nod, glancing around the cozy bakery adorned with holiday decorations. "It's been busy, but I can't complain. The holiday season always brings a special kind of magic to this place."

Madden's eyes take in the festive scene, and he offers a genuine compliment. "You've done an incredible job with the holiday decorations. This place looks amazing."

Grinning with pride, I reply, "Thank you, Madden. It's my favorite time of the year, and I love sharing that festive spirit with the town."

We delve into small talk for a moment, a welcome break from the whirlwind of the holiday season. He updates me on how the resort's reopening is progressing, the challenges he's faced, and the dedication of the staff working tirelessly to make it a success. It's a moment to connect on a more personal level, away from the business responsibilities that have been defining our interactions lately.

I listen as he speaks, and I can't help but appreciate his genuine interest taking over the ski resort. "It's a lot of work," he admits with a sigh, "but I'm determined to make the resort thrive again."

I offer a supportive smile, and encouraging words, "I have no doubt you'll do an amazing job, Madden. You've always been dedicated to everything you do."

"Thank you, Aaliyah. It means a lot coming from you," he says.

Our conversation meanders for a while, touching on various topics, from the holiday season to the joys of our small town. We share stories, anecdotes, and even a few moments of laughter. It's a reminder of the easy rapport that has developed between us, a friendship that has grown stronger despite the years that separated us.

My gaze drifts to the Christmas decorations outside the bakery, and I can't help but feel a sense of gratitude for my hometown. The subject of the town's Christmas festival comes up. I explain the various preparations that are underway, from the Christmas tree lighting ceremony to the festive market that will line the streets. It's a time when the whole town comes together to celebrate the season, and the sense of community is palpable.

Madden's gaze lingers on the decorations outside. "It sounds wonderful. As I look around, I remember why this time of year is so special here. I can tell though that it has gotten more popular since I have been gone. I didn't really come home to much through the years after I finished college."

I nod, "It truly is. The holiday season here is magical. Now you can be a part of the festivities. You know your parents have always made the ski resort a main attraction for the holidays."

"Yea, I heard. The manager and the staff are taking care of all of it this year. I told them that I really wasn't ready to dive into this year. Mom on the other hand said that it was dad's favorite time of year and he prided himself on decorating the ski resort, so she is planning with the staff and helping to decorate it. I am however, helping her decorate the house," he says.

"That's good for the both of you," I tell him.

Then, unexpectedly, the conversation shifts to the town's Christmas festival and the Christmas Eve dance, a tradition that has always brought the community together. "You know about the other another holiday tradition my mom mentioned to me yesterday, the Christmas Eve dance that the town hosts every year. She said that it brings the community together, a night of music, dancing, and celebration," he says and before

I can reply he looks at me with a glint of mischief in his eyes and says, "Aaliyah, I was wondering if you'd be my date to the Christmas Eve dance."

The question catches me off guard, and I find myself momentarily stunned. It's an invitation I hadn't expected, and my heart quickens with a mix of excitement and uncertainty. Is he asking me as a friend, or could this be a genuine date?

I take a moment to collect my thoughts, my gaze meeting his. "Well, Madden, I'd be honored to be your date to the Christmas Eve dance."

His smile widens, and it's a heartwarming sight. "Great. I'm looking forward to it."

As he leaves the bakery, I'm left with a whirlwind of emotions. I've accepted his invitation with a mixture of curiosity and hope, though I can't quite shake the notion that perhaps he's asking me as a friend.

* * *

As the evening sky paints the town in shades of dusky blue, I begin the process of closing up my bakery. The cozy, warm interior takes on a softer glow as the decorative lights twinkle around the room, casting a gentle radiance that adds to the bakery's charm. The aroma of freshly baked treats lingers in the air, a comforting reminder of the day's busy but successful operations.

The last customer leaves with a contented smile, the bell above the door chiming softly as they exit. I follow them with a warm farewell and a wish for a joyful evening. With a contented sigh, I step behind the counter, ready to tidy up, lock up, and bring the day to a close.

It's moments like these that I treasure, the quiet interlude as I prepare to end the day. The hustle and bustle of the holiday season seems a world away, replaced by a sense of calm that washes over me. There's a certain magic in this transition, as the bakery transforms from a bustling hub of activity to a serene haven.

One by one, I start to switch off the decorative lights, allowing the soft ambient lighting to illuminate the room. I glance at the display case, the trays of pastries, and the rows of cupcakes that have graced the counter tops throughout the day. It's been a day filled with the joy of sharing my passion for baking, and now, as I prepare to close, it feels like a quiet, intimate moment between me and my bakery.

Once the bakery is tidied and secured for the night, I slip into my coat and scarf, the chilly December air brushing against my cheeks as I step outside. The town is aglow with the soft illumination of holiday lights, casting a dreamlike quality over the town. The streets are adorned with decorations that evoke a sense of nostalgia, and I can't help but smile as I stroll through the familiar surroundings. The storefronts showcase festive displays, and the windows are alive with the spirit of the season. The scent of pine and cinnamon wafts from the Christmas trees that line the streets, their branches twinkling with an array of ornaments and lights.

People bustle about, their laughter and conversations filling the air with a sense of community. Children's eyes light up with wonder as they gaze at the holiday displays, and couples walk hand in hand, embracing the romantic atmosphere that envelops the town.

I find myself captivated by the warm and inviting ambiance, taking in every detail as I make my way through the town. The soft crunch of snow underfoot adds to the winter wonderland experience, and I can't help but feel like a character in a holiday storybook.

As I walk, my thoughts drift back to Madden and the Christmas Eve dance. It's a surprising development, one that fills me with curiosity and excitement. I still can't help but wonder about the nature of his invitation. Is it as friends, as we have been building our connection, or is there something more to it? The uncertainty adds a layer of intrigue to the upcoming event.

With a contented heart, I continue to stroll through the town, soaking in the holiday spirit. This is a special time of year, a time to celebrate and to appreciate the bonds we share with our neighbors and friends. The town's festive preparations have created an enchanting backdrop for the holiday season.

Chapter Eight

Madden

The soft glow of the desk lamp casts a warm ambiance over the room, its light flickering like a beacon in the stillness of the night. I've always found solace in my father's office, a place that holds the memories of my father and my grandfather, the legacy that now rests on my shoulders. It brings back so many good memories of family, pain and heartbreak.

Sitting in what is now my office on a quiet Saturday evening, I find my thoughts drifting to Aaliyah and the unexpected turn of events. Her agreement to accompany me to the Christmas Eve dance lingers in my mind, a source of both anticipation and trepidation. This is something that I wanted as a high school teenager; to ask Aaliyah Evans out on a date. It took me a really long time to finally have opportunity and I couldn't pass it up. I am excited and nervous about our date to the dance. It makes me feel like that young teenage boy again. The only difference now is that I have a lot of experience, knowledge, and even some dark secrets and desires that she has no idea about.

As I think about Aaliyah, a soft smile tugs at the corners of my lips. There's an undeniable connection that has grown between us, a sense of comfort in her presence. Her grace and charm have captivated me in a way I hadn't anticipated, and the prospect of the Christmas Eve dance is both exciting and daunting.

But as the smile fades, I can't help but acknowledge the shadow of uncertainty that looms over me. It's not about the dance itself or our growing friendship, but rather the secret desires and the enigmatic past that I've kept hidden. Aaliyah is a woman of grace and sophistication, someone who embodies a sense of elegance that transcends the ordinary. She's a woman who exudes charm and warmth, and I can't help but wonder if my hidden desires and the darkness that I've concealed will be too much for her to accept.

My gaze drifts to a small, locked drawer in my desk, the repository of secrets that have remained hidden from the world. It contains the key to a world I've explored in the shadows, a world of dominance and submission that goes far beyond the norms of conventional relationships. It's a side of me that few have glimpsed, a facet of my identity that I've chosen to keep hidden. The memories of my time in New York resurface, a city that had offered both power and anonymity. It was there that I had delved into the world of dominance and submission, a world where control and submission danced in a delicate balance. It had been a realm that allowed me to explore my deepest desires, a part of me that I had kept hidden even from those closest to me.

The secrets that had unfolded in those dimly lit rooms, the

trust that had been exchanged between Dom and sub. They were experiences that had shaped me in profound ways. But they were also experiences that had been shrouded in secrecy, concealed beneath the veneer of my life as a powerful attorney.

When you compare my two worlds, they have been a delicate dance, a tightrope walking between two identities. On one hand, I was the driven attorney, successful and composed, and on the other, I was the man who had explored the complexities of dominance and submission.

* * *

I remember that night vividly, the night that I attended my first play party in New York City, a night that would forever alter the course of my life and lead to a profound self-discovery. The memories of the scenes I witnessed that evening are etched in my mind, moments that unveiled the truth about my desires and the revelation of my identity as a Dom. It really takes me back to a piece of me that I know I can never bury and not let out.

The invitation to my first play party came from an unexpected source, a fellow attorney at the law firm where I worked in New York. His name was Elliot, a colleague I had known for a few years. Elliot was a charismatic and enigmatic figure in the legal world, known for his sharp mind and a penchant for maintaining a life beyond the confines of the office.

It was during a casual conversation in the break room that he broached the subject. His tone was conspiratorial, his eyes filled with a mischievous glint. He mentioned the play party in hushed tones, alluding to a world of secrets and desires that lay hidden from the prying eyes of the legal world. Elliot said that he had sensed something in me, a curiosity that I had always kept concealed. He had observed the way I navigated the complexities of the legal field, the air of authority and control that I exuded. It was as if he had seen a part of me that I had never revealed to anyone.

With a sly smile, he extended the invitation, his words laced with the promise of an experience that would forever alter my perception of desire and control. He spoke of a world where power dynamics reigned, where trust and surrender held a unique beauty. I hesitated at first, uncertain of what lay ahead, but the allure of the unknown drew me in. The world of Dominance and submission that Elliot described resonated with something deep within me, a truth about my desires that I could no longer ignore. It was Elliot who had opened the door to this hidden realm, the world of the play party, and it was a gesture that would lead to the revelation of my true identity as a Dom.

The play party was held in a discreet, dimly lit venue that exuded an air of sensuality and anticipation. As I stepped into the room, I was greeted by an atmosphere of intrigue and allure. The space was adorned with red velvet drapes, soft, evocative lighting, and an array of implements that hinted at the adventures that would unfold.

One of the first scenes that caught my attention was a mesmerizing display of rope bondage. A woman was suspended from the ceiling, her body intricately bound with ropes that created a striking web of lines and knots. Her skin glistened with sweat as she dangled in the air, her body arched in a pose of vulnerability and trust. The Dom, a skilled rigger, moved with precision and grace as he manipulated the ropes, his every movement deliberate and controlled. The connection between them was palpable, a dance of trust and surrender that held the room in rapt attention. As I watched the scene unfold, I couldn't tear my gaze away. The woman's surrender was a testament to her trust in her Dom, and the Dom's expertise was a display of control and mastery. It was a moment of profound beauty and intensity, a moment that resonated with something deep within me. The realization struck me like a lightning bolt, I was drawn to the dynamics of power and submission, to the intricate balance of control and surrender. It was a truth about myself that I could no longer deny, a revelation that left me both exhilarated and apprehensive.

The second scene that left a lasting impact on me was an intense session of impact play. A submissive, her skin adorned with delicate red marks from previous strikes, knelt before her Dom. The Dom held a flogger in his hand, its tails swaying with a sense of purpose. With each strike, the submissive's body quivered, and a delicate moan escaped her lips. The Dom's movements were deliberate and controlled, and there was a certain rhythm to the way he wielded the flogger. The connection between them was undeniable, a dance of pleasure and pain that transcended the physical sensations. I found myself captivated by the scene, the complexity of the emotions on display, and the trust that existed between the participants. It was a moment of vulnerability and intensity, a moment that revealed the depths of their desires.

As I watched, I felt a resonance within me, a recognition of the desires that had always simmered beneath the surface. I realized that I was drawn to the power dynamics, to the intricate interplay of control and submission, and to the trust that existed between Dom and submissive. It was in the midst of those scenes, amid the beauty and intensity of the play party, that I acknowledged a truth about myself that I could no longer ignore, I was a Dom. The desire to control and lead, to guide and protect, had always existed within me, hidden beneath the surface of the successful attorney I had become.

Chapter Eight

* * *

Now, sitting in my office in the town I had once left behind, I can't help but wonder how these hidden secrets will impact my burgeoning connection with Aaliyah. The prospect of the Christmas Eve dance with Aaliyah is a step into an unknown future, a future where I'm forced to confront the secrets, I've kept hidden.

It's a moment that fills me with both longing and concern, a moment that will reveal whether Aaliyah can accept the hidden facets of my desires and the enigmatic past that I've concealed. In the silence of my office, the weight of my hidden secrets presses down on me, leaving me to wonder whether the darkness within me can coexist with the light of the connection I'm building with her.

Chapter Nine

Aaliyah

The anticipation has been building for weeks, and today is the day of the Christmas Eve dance, a moment that fills me with a mix of excitement and nervousness. The bakery is my pride and joy, but I've made arrangements for Rene to handle the bakery for the remainder of the day and the closing duties so that I can leave early and prepare for the evening ahead.

"Rene, I am fixing to head out," I yell to her in the back of the store.

Rene walks through the door from the back storage and says, "Don't worry about things here. I have it all taken care of. You go and enjoy yourself. I for one am rooting for you and Madden to become more than just friends!"

"First of all, thank you for taking care of the store for me. Second, I think you are way off base about me and Madden," I tell her.

"I am not blind! I see the way both of you look at each other," Rene replies with a giggle. "Now, get out of here. Go home and put on that beautiful gown Cinderella and don't forget your glass slippers!"

I have to laugh at that point and couldn't come back with a reply. I just continue laughing as I walk out of the front door.

The sun is beginning to dip below the horizon. I head home, eager to start getting ready. I've spent a good amount of time pondering over what to wear, the dilemma of choosing the perfect outfit. In the end, I opt for a deep crimson dress that drapes elegantly, accentuating my figure. It feels like a fitting choice for the occasion, one that matches the festive atmosphere of the holiday dance.

As I stand before the mirror, applying a touch of makeup and arranging my hair, I can't help but think about the evening ahead. Madden had asked me to be his date, and the thought of spending the night with him is both thrilling and nerve-wracking. He's seen me in my everyday attire, but tonight, he'll see a different side of me, all dressed up for the dance.

When I see his car pull up in front of my house, I'm greeted with a look of genuine surprise and appreciation on Madden's face. His gaze lingers on me, and his smile is like a warm embrace that dispels any remaining nervousness. It's a reassuring reaction, and I can't help but feel a sense of confidence wash over me.

The dress I've chosen seems to have earned his approval, and the unspoken admiration in his eyes is a welcome sight. It's a small, yet significant moment, one that makes me feel like I've made the right choice. His reaction is a testament to the effort I've put into getting ready for the evening.

"Wow," he says, his voice carrying a hint of admiration. "You look amazing, Aaliyah."

A smile tugs at the corners of my lips, and I can't help but feel a rush of warmth at his words. "Thank you," I reply, feeling a touch of bashfulness. "I wanted to make sure I looked the part for this special night."

His gaze lingers on me, and the sincerity in his eyes is unmistakable. It's a look that goes beyond mere politeness, a look that seems to say he genuinely appreciates the effort I've put into getting ready. It's a reassuring reaction, one that eases any lingering nerves I might have had.

"You more than succeeded," he remarks with a grin, and it's a compliment that fills me with a sense of pride.

"Well thank you Sir. You look very dashing yourself," I tell him, and I was not lying. This man for as long as I can remember, has been the most handsome man I have ever known and when he came back into this town and into my life a few short weeks ago, he still took my breath away.

He smiled at me, then opened my car door and let me slip inside. Before he shut the door and walked to his side of the car, he looks at me with a spark in his eyes and says, "You are the most beautiful women in the world."

* * *

When we get into town, we park the car at the bakery and decide to walk to the high school through town. On our way as we walk the streets they are bathed in the soft, enchanting glow of holiday lights. The atmosphere is filled with the spirit of the season, and it feels as if we're walking through a winter wonderland. We pause to admire the festive displays, the decorations that bring a touch of magic to the town. We stop at the big Christmas tree in the center of town where parents have their kids waiting in a line to see Santa and his elves to sit on his lap and give him their Christmas list and take a photo. We watch as the kids run up to his lap and listen to all the laughter they are making.

We continue our walk and stop at the park where there is an adult play going on. We stop and watch the remainder of it. At the end the carolers in the play sing *Oh Holy Night* and the crowd joins in and sings with them. As the play comes to its close, we start to walk the rest of the way to the high school along with most of the crowd.

When we get to the school and the gym comes into comes into view, its entrance bathed in the soft twinkle of fairy light. The music can be heard even from outside, a lively melody that beckons us inside. As we step through the doors, it has been transformed for the occasion. The dance floor is alive with couples twirling and swaying to the rhythm. The sound of laughter and the warmth of the crowd envelop us.

Madden and I make our way to the dance floor, and as we start to move to the music, the world around us fades into the background. It's as if it's just the two of us, lost in the moment. The connection between us deepens with each step, and I find myself drawn to his presence.

We talk and laugh, sharing stories about the dances we had been to and the sports games we had played in or attended in this very gym. I feel like I'm getting to know him on a deeper level. The evening unfolds with a sense of joy and intimacy, a night that exceeds my expectations. The dance is the perfect backdrop for us to connect, to explore the chemistry that has been growing between us.

As the night unfolds and we dance, Madden surprises me

with a question that fills me with warmth. He leans in, his eyes sincere, and asks, "Aaliyah, would you be willing to spend Christmas Day with me and my mom?"

I pause for a moment, a sense of delight and anticipation washing over me. "Christmas Day?" I repeat, feeling my excitement grow. "I'd be honored, Madden. That sounds like a wonderful way to spend the holiday."

His smile is genuine, and I can see the relief in his eyes, as if he's truly pleased by my response. "I'm really glad you said yes. I think you'll love my mom, and she's been looking forward to meeting you."

The idea of spending Christmas with Madden and his mom fills me with a sense of connection and belonging. It's more than just a holiday invitation; it feels like a significant step in our budding relationship.

When the dance comes to a close, Madden and I walk back to his car. It's a chilly night, and he offers me his coat, a small act of chivalry that makes my heart flutter. As we reach his car, he once again opens my door like the gentleman that he is.

We pull up back at my house and he gets out of the car and comes to let me out. Then he walks me to my front door. The chill in the air is a reminder of the winter night, but it's a gentle backdrop to the warmth between us. We stand on the doorstep, and I turn to face him, a soft smile on my lips. "Thank you for the wonderful evening, Madden. I had an amazing time."

His gaze is filled with appreciation as he replies, "Aaliyah, the pleasure was all mine. You made tonight special."

I feel a touch of shyness but decide to speak my mind. "I'm really looking forward to spending Christmas Day with you and your mom."

His eyes light up, and he reaches for my hand, holding it

gently. "I am too, Aaliyah. It will be a great pleasure to have you spend Christmas with us."

A sense of contentment washes over me, and I feel a growing connection between us. It's a moment charged with unspoken emotions, and I decide to take a step closer. Our faces are just inches apart, and I can feel the warmth of his breath. Madden leans in, and his lips meet mine in a soft, yet passionate kiss. It's a moment of tenderness and desire, a promise of the moments we'll share in the days to come.

As he pulls away, our eyes meet, and I can't help but smile. "Goodnight, Madden," I say, my voice filled with a sense of anticipation.

"Goodnight, Aaliyah," he replies, his tone filled with warmth. "I'll see you tomorrow at 3 pm."

With that, he takes a step back and watches me as I open the door and step inside. A sense of contentment and anticipation filling my heart. The Christmas dance has been a night to remember, a night that has deepened the connection between us and set the stage for the holiday season ahead.

Chapter Ten

Madden

Early in the morning on Christmas Day, I find myself waking up to the wonderful aroma of my mom's cooking. The scent of roast turkey, savory stuffing, and all the traditional holiday dishes fills the house. I can hear her humming softly as she moves about the kitchen, a comforting sound that stirs a sense of nostalgia. Hearing her in the kitchen humming and enjoying her time cooking Christmas dinner made me smile. I am glad that she is able to laugh and smile. I know that she still has her moments since dad's passing, and I know that she always will but knowing that she is still living life and enjoying some sense of normalcy makes me feel better. I know me being here and taking over the family business takes some of the weight and worry off of her too.

Thinking about taking over the family business, while I am in New York for New Year's Eve, I have to sit down with the partners of the firm and tell them that I am not coming back.

That is one meeting that I am not eager to have. Mainly because it is not a decision that I wanted to make.

As I prepare to walk downstairs to see Mom being the master in the kitchen that she has always been. The holidays are her time to shine. I can picture her with her apron on, a dash of flour on her cheek, and a smile on her face as she prepares a feast fit for the season. It's a tradition that's been a part of our family for as long as I can remember, and it's something I've missed during my years in New York.

As the morning turns into early afternoon, I can hardly contain my excitement as I wait on Aaliyah to arrive. I've been looking forward to spending this special day with her. I've been helping my mom with the final preparations, setting the table and making sure everything is just right.

As the clock ticks toward 3 pm, Aaliyah's arrival is met with eager anticipation. I can hardly contain my excitement as I hear the doorbell ring, and I rush to open the door. Aaliyah stands there, a vision of beauty, holding a bundle of delicious treats in her hands. My heart does a little dance at the sight of her.

"Hi, Madden," she greets me with a warm smile, her eyes sparkling with happiness.

"Hey, Aaliyah," I reply, matching her smile. "You look amazing."

Her cheeks tint with a hint of bashfulness. "Thank you. I wanted to bring a little something for your Christmas dinner."

With a grin, I lead her inside, and she's immediately greeted by the wonderful aroma of my mom's cooking. Mom appears from the kitchen, an apron wrapped around her, and her eyes light up when she sees Aaliyah.

"Madden, dear, is this the lovely Aaliyah?" she asks with an inviting smile.

I nod with enthusiasm. "Yes, Mom, it's Aaliyah. Aaliyah, this is my mom, Clara."

Aaliyah and my mom exchange warm greetings, and it's clear that they're getting along right from the start. They chat like old friends, and the atmosphere is filled with genuine camaraderie. It warms my heart to see them bonding so easily.

As we settle down at the dinner table, it's like a picture-perfect Christmas scene. The table is adorned with festive decorations, and the dishes are a delicious sight to behold. There's turkey, stuffing, cranberry sauce, and all the traditional favorites that make this holiday special.

Over dinner, conversation flows naturally. Aaliyah shares stories from her life, and my mom listens with genuine interest. The laughter and shared moments make it feel like a real family gathering.

Once the plates are cleared, it's time for dessert, and Aaliyah unveils the array of treats she's brought two cakes, banana pudding, fudge, and a delightful assortment of cookies. The dessert table is a sight to behold, and I can see the appreciation in my mom's eyes.

As the evening progresses, there's a moment I've been eagerly waiting for. I reach for a small, wrapped gift that I've hidden in the corner of the room and hand it to Aaliyah. She looks surprised, and a hint of guilt crosses her expression.

"You didn't have to get me anything," she says, a touch of regret in her voice.

I offer her a reassuring smile. "It's not about the gift, Aaliyah. It's about the sentiment."

She unwraps the package to find a cheerleader figurine wearing a snowsuit. It's a small token, but I hope it conveys what I want to say. "I wanted to give you something that reminded me of you – someone who brings cheer and warmth into my life."

Aaliyah's eyes meet mine, and there's a moment of hesitation before she finally responds, her voice filled with emotion, "Madden, I didn't get you anything. I feel terrible."

I shake my head, assuring her, "Don't worry about that. Aaliyah, I've enjoyed spending time with you, and I have to admit, I'm starting to have real feelings for you, more than just a friend."

The room is filled with a hushed silence, and Aaliyah's voice is gentle but filled with emotion as she replies, "Madden, I love it. Thank you so much and I feel the same way about you."

It's a moment that fills me with happiness and relief. We've both acknowledged our growing connection, and the feeling of knowing that we're on the same page is incredibly reassuring.

As the evening winds down, Mom has turned in for the evening and Aaliyah and I have finished cleaning up the kitchen. We sit in front of the fireplace sipping on some more wine. I know that now is the time to talk to her about something that's been on my mind. With the cozy warmth of the fire, I take a deep breath and turn to her, ready to broach a different subject.

"Aaliyah," I begin, "I have something I need to talk to you about."

She looks at me with a curious expression, her eyes still reflecting the joy of the day. "Sure, Madden. What is it?"

I meet her gaze, my voice filled with sincerity. "I need to go back to New York and talk to the partners at the law firm. I have to let them know that I'm not coming back."

Aaliyah's brows furrow in surprise, and she asks, "You're not going back to New York?"

I nod, my thoughts focused. "That's right. I've decided to stay in Ouray, and I'm going to run the ski resort with my mom. It's time for me to be here with her."

Aaliyah's expression shifts, a mix of understanding and support in her eyes. "Madden, I think that's a wonderful decision. Your mom will appreciate having you here."

I appreciate her encouragement and continue, "There's also the matter of my condo in New York. I'll need to figure out what to do with it."

Her voice is filled with understanding as she says, "You can take your time to decide. It's a big step, but it's clear that your heart is here in Ouray."

I smile, grateful for her understanding. Then, I decide to share my other proposition. "Aaliyah, there's a New Year's Eve party in New York that I thought you might like to attend. It's going to be an incredible event, and I'd love for you to come with me. You deserve a vacation. Just take a few days off. We fly out on Wednesday night. I meet with my partners on Thursday morning. After that the rest of the weekend is ours. We can sight see and enjoy the ball dropping on New Years Eve before heading to the party. It's my treat!"

She looks at me, her eyes reflecting the exhaustion from the day's celebrations but also a glimmer of interest. "New Year's in New York? That sounds amazing. And you are right, I could use a vacation. I would love to come! I will talk to Rene and have her run the bakery. "

I can see the joy in her eyes as she agrees, and it fills me with a sense of excitement. We sit for another hour just enjoying the ambiance of the fire before she decides it is time for her to go home. I walk her to her car and kiss her goodnight.

I go to sleep thinking about the events of the last few days. As I think about the trip to New York and the New Year's Eve

Chapter Ten

party that will open her eyes to my darkest secrets and desires, I can only hope that she will not run away and will at least give it some thought and join me in my desires. It is weird. I can usually tell immediately if a woman is a sub or not, but with Aaliyah, I just can't tell. I don't know if my radar is off because of my feelings for her or if maybe she is hiding her true self.

Chapter Eleven

Madden

L eaving for New York with Aaliyah fills me with a sense of anticipation. Our flight leaves on Wednesday night and return the flight is scheduled for Sunday night, but for now, I'm focused on the adventures awaiting us. I am hoping that this trip will be not only a memorable New Year's Eve experience for us and our budding relationship, but one that will allow her into my world; a world that I hope she will accept and be a part of.

As the day of our departure arrives, I can't help but feel a sense of excitement mixed with anticipation. Picking up Aaliyah from her house, I arrive with a knock on her door. When she opens it, I'm greeted by her radiant smile, and it warms my heart. She's all set to go, dressed in a way that makes her look even more captivating. She is wearing a pair of jeans, snow boots, a pink sweater that looks absolutely amazing with her skin tone.

"Ready for this adventure?" I ask as I offer a hand to help

with her luggage.

Aaliyah nods with enthusiasm, her eyes shining. "Absolutely, Madden. I can't wait. Let me grab my coat and make sure all the lights are off and I will lock up and be right out."

"Okay, I will put your luggage in the car," I tell her as she runs back inside the house.

I load her bags into the car, and I can sense the energy of the trip. We make small talk as we drive to the airport, sharing anecdotes and stories about our previous trips and travel experiences. The car ride is filled with a sense of anticipation for what awaits us in New York.

When we arrive at the airport, the bustling terminal is alive with people ready to embark on their own adventures. We check in and make our way to the gate. We stop and get chips and a soda to have while we wait on our flight to be called.

Once they call our boarding passes, we get on the plane, and find our seats, as the hum of the engines fills the cabin. We settle into our seats, and I can't help but feel nervous and excited about sharing this part of my life with her. The flight brings us closer to our destination, but it also offers us time to relax and enjoy each other's company. I turn to Aaliyah, my voice warm as I say, "Aaliyah, I'm so glad you decided to come with me. This trip is going to be unforgettable."

She smiles, her eyes reflecting the same sentiment. "I'm excited, Madden. Thank you for inviting me. I can't wait to see what New York has in store for us."

As the plane takes off, we settle into our seats and just chat about the beautiful sky and watch a movie on the TV in the headrests.

We arrive in Manhattan, and I take her to my home. Aaliyah is staying in the guest room, but I want her to feel comfortable and at home in my space. I drop off our bags in our rooms and we head back into the living room.

"It has been a long day. I am starving. Let's go to this restaurant I know down the street for dinner," I say.

"That sounds great. I am starving," she replies.

We get to the restaurant and the ambiance of our first dinner in the city is nothing short of enchanting. I took her to my favorite little restaurant not far from my condo. It's a cozy, downtown Manhattan restaurant with a romantic atmosphere. Soft lighting and the gentle glow of candles create an intimate setting, and the aroma of delicious cuisine fills the air.

We clink our wine glasses, savoring the moment, as I can't help but appreciate the beauty of the evening. Aaliyah's eyes light up as she takes in the surroundings, and her smile is infectious. The city has a unique charm, and it's clear that she's thrilled to be here.

"New York is truly amazing," she says with genuine enthusiasm. "I'm so glad I took the time off to come. I've always wanted to see this city."

Her excitement is a breath of fresh air, and I'm grateful to share this experience with her. We talk about the places she's eager to visit, the sights she's always dreamed of seeing over dinner.

When we get back to my condo, we retreat to our rooms for the night. As I lay there in my bed alone, I can't help but get a hard on thinking about her being in the next room. I think about what if anything she is wearing to bed. I think about what it would feel like to have her in the bed with me; how she would feel under me and how she would feel with me inside of her. *Damn, I need a release.* I have no choice but to do it myself. I lay there and jack my dick thinking about her.

* * *

On Thursday, it's time for me to meet with my partners and have a conversation that I've been preparing for. There's also a hint of nervousness simmering beneath the surface. I can't help but think about the life I'm leaving behind in the city, the life of a prestigious attorney that I've carefully cultivated.

As Aaliyah and I share a cup of coffee at the breakfast table, I take a moment to voice my concerns. "I am having a lot of emotions this morning." I confess, "There is a part of me that doesn't want to quit my job and leave the big city. I worked hard to build a life here that I wanted. But I also have come to realize that not only does my mom need me, but I have missed being home in Ouray. I am looking forward to continuing the family business and what life there now has to offer me."

She gazes at me with understanding in her eyes. "I can imagine how hard that must be for you, Madden. It's a big step. But know that you mom and I will be here as you make this change. It is normal for you to have these feelings. The good thing is that you recognize them."

I nod, my voice tinged with a mix of apprehension and determination. "It is. I've spent years building my career in the city, but I've come to realize that my heart is in Ouray. It's time for a change."

After breakfast, I proceed to the meeting with my partners. As I sit across from them, I can't help but feel the weight of my decision. The conversation unfolds with sincerity, and I tell them that I won't be returning to the firm. I explain my desire to run the ski resort with my mom and the need to be closer to family.

My partners listen with empathy, and I can see that they

understand how hard this decision is for me. They offer their best wishes and express their support. Their understanding and well-wishes make this transition a little easier to bear.

I get back home, and Aaliyah is sitting on the sofa watching a movie on Lifetime. It only takes that one scene to let me know that I made the right decision.

She heard me come and turns around as asks, "How did it go and how do you feel?"

I walk up, sit beside her on the couch, lean in and give her a kiss. When I pull back, I say, "It went well. They were understanding and sad to see me go. As to how I feel that kiss says it all. Now I have a surprise for you." I pull out of my jacket pocket a small envelope and hand it to her.

She looks at me with curiosity as she takes the envelope and opens it. When she pulls out the two tickets to Beauty and the Beast on Broadway, she squeals in joy. "Oh my god! Madden I never thought that you would get us tickets! I was just mentioning it as something I had on my bucket list to do one day!"

"Today is one day!" I tell her.

She jumps over to me, throws her arms around my neck and pulls me in for a kiss. She tries to back away with just a quick little kiss, but I can't let her go. I want more. I am tired of the just friendly kisses. I put my hand on the back of her head and pull her back in and press my tongue between her lips with force opening her mouth up for me to devour.

I move my hands from her head to the front of her sweater. My mouth leaves her mouth and trails kisses over her neck. She moans in response. I pull her sweater up over her head and throw it on the floor. I unsnap her black lace bra and throw it on the floor too and then lay her back on the couch.

She looks into my eyes and says, "Madden, I....," but I stop her by covering my mouth over hers again.

Whatever she was going to say, I knew it would be along the lines of we shouldn't. But I couldn't stop. I want to please her and taste her, and I can't wait any longer. While kissing her, I remove her jeans and my hands feel the lace of her thongs as I pull them off next. I can only imagine they are the same as her black bra that I took off just a few minutes ago.

I lift up and trail kisses down to her breasts, sucking and licking around her nipples from one breast to another. I ran the palm of my hand over her pussy to find it already dripping wet. I slip two fingers inside of her and pump them in and out in rhythm while still sucking her nipples from one breast to the other. She starts rising her hips and I know that she wants more than just my fingers.

I slip my fingers out of her and lift up just slightly so I can see her eyes. I rise my fingers to my mouth and suck her juices off of them. Damn she tastes so good. I lean down and kiss her again opening her mouth and sticking my tongue inside so that she can see how good she tastes too.

Then I slide down her body and lift her legs over my shoulders and lick her sweet spot. I bite down on her clit slightly. Then I stick my tongue inside of her. I continue to penetrate with my tongue and then lick and suck until she is almost ready to come. I take my index finger and stick it inside her ass and pump as I continue to devour her sweet pussy until she comes in a loud scream of pleasure. I lick up every drop. I sit up and look at her laying on my couch like a beautiful, sated angel.

"Come on. We both have to get ready for tonight. Before the show we are going to dinner," I tell her.

She looks up at me with a confused look that I immediately

recognized.

"Don't worry, we will continue this later," I tell her.

She smiles and I help her off the couch and pick up her clothes. We head upstairs to get ready for our evening.

We head out to dinner and then to a Broadway play. The night is filled with the magic of the theater, and we share our thoughts and impressions during the intermission. After the show we go back to the house, and we head to our rooms for the night.

* * *

Friday is a day of sightseeing, and I'm excited to show Aaliyah the iconic places in the city. We explore Central Park, visit the Empire State Building, and take a stroll along Times Square. Our conversations flow easily, and we share stories and laughter as we take in the sights. But as Friday comes to an end, I get more and more nervous about New Year's Eve night.

Chapter Twelve

Madden

Saturday finally arrives. I have been excited and nervous about this day since I asked Aaliyah to come to New York with me and attend a New Year's Eve party. I still wasn't sure how to bring it all up to her. Should I just take her to the party with no warning as to what type of party it is or prepare her in some way or another? I am so confused as to how to handle it and now it is the day of, and I have to decide.

Once I step out of my bedroom door, I smell bacon, coffee and something sweet coming from the kitchen. *Man, the woman is cooking us breakfast! When did she go to the store?*

"Wow! It smells so good in here. My stomach is growling!" I say as I walk into the kitchen.

"I hope you enjoy it! I wanted to do something nice for you. Early this morning I had some food delivered for breakfast and lunch so that I can cook for you!" she said as she pours me a cup of coffee.

"Thank you," I say as she hands me my coffee and I lean forward and kiss her gently on the lips. "I am sure I will enjoy it all," I continue after the kiss.

She giggles like a schoolgirl and says, "It will be ready in a few minutes. I have bacon, sausage, banana pancakes, scrambled eggs, strawberry crepes, and hash browns."

"Sounds amazing. Are you going to tell me what we are having for lunch?" I ask.

"No! It's another surprise!" she laughs out.

Breakfast was amazing as so was the homemade lasagna she made for lunch. We spend the remainder of the day relaxing in each other's arms watching TV until it was time for us to get ready to head out to see the ball drop. Of course, it is still hours before it drops, but I want her to be able to experience the whole event.

* * *

Times Square is ablaze with the brilliant, dazzling lights that have become iconic symbols of New Year's Eve. As Aaliyah and I make our way through the bustling crowds, the energy in the air is palpable. The artist on the stage, a talented singer, fills the square with music that reverberates through our very bones. The music, a backdrop to the sea of people, surrounds us with a sense of unity and excitement, as if we're all part of this collective celebration.

The lights above, the massive screens displaying the countdown, and the enthusiastic chatter of the crowd make this experience unlike any other. As we navigate the throngs of people, I can't help but be amazed by the sheer magnitude of it all. It's a celebration on a grand scale, a reminder of the passage of time and the promise of a new year.

As the clock inches closer to midnight, the anticipation in the crowd is electric. Aaliyah's hand in mine, I can feel her excitement, her heart beating in rhythm with the countdown. We look up at the ball, a shimmering sphere of hope and dreams, ready to drop and mark the beginning of a new chapter.

Ten... nine... eight...

The voices of the crowd unite in a collective cheer, counting down to the final moments of the year. It's a cacophony of joy, a celebration of life, and a reminder that we're all part of something bigger.

Three... two... one...

The ball drops, and at that precise moment, as the world erupts in celebration, I turn to Aaliyah. Amidst the cheers and confetti that rains down on us, her eyes meet mine, and in that instant, I know there's no place I'd rather be. With all the passion that's been building between us, I lean in, capturing her lips with mine. The kiss is filled with promise and hope of a newfound relationship.

The party is only a few blocks from Time Square. As we are walking, to the party, I know that I have to tell Aaliyah that there are some aspects of my life in New York that I want to share with her.

"Aaliyah, there is something that I need to tell you before we get to the party. This party is not a typical New Year's Eve party. It represents some aspects of my life, my private life that I don't share with a lot of people. I want to ask you to just keep an open mind," I tell her. "I think letting you see it for yourself will be better than me just telling you."

I can see the curiosity in her eyes, but she doesn't ask any questions, just shakes her head yes.

When we arrive at the party, at first, seems like a typical New Year's celebration, but as we step inside, the atmosphere changes. I can sense the moment when Aaliyah realizes that it's more than just a regular party.

There are people standing everywhere, some still dressed in their best party dresses and tuxes, and some are down to their lingerie and leather, while others are naked. I see her eyes go big, but she still doesn't say anything.

We walk further in and in the back, there is a California King bed. There is a man in leather pants with a riding whip in his hand. His sub is bent over the edge of the bed with her hands tied in front of her and strapped to the chains coming from the head of the bed. He is taking the whip and landing it across her ass.

There are various groups of people at the engaged in BDSM activities and some just watching and not participating. I watch her expressions as she realizes what is going on and what I have kept hidden for a long time. I can see the mix of emotions in her eyes, curiosity, surprise, and perhaps a hint of uncertainty.

As Aaliyah and I move through the dimly lit rooms of the BDSM party, we witness scenes that offer glimpses into the diverse and intricate world of dominance and submission. The air is heavy with anticipation, and each scene unfolds with its own intensity and unique dynamics.

We continue to walk around the room and come to one corner of the room where a Dom stands tall, his commanding presence undeniable. He is impeccably dressed in leather, exuding an air of authority. Before him, a submissive partner kneels, their vulnerability and trust evident. It's a tableau of power exchange, a dance of submission, and dominance. The submissive, a vision of vulnerability and trust, kneels before the Dom. She wears a tight-fitting, black leather corset and matching cuffs, accentuating the contours of her body. Her gaze remains fixed on the ground, a symbol of her submission and unwavering trust in her Dom. With meticulous care, the Dom selects a set of implements, each one meticulously chosen for its specific purpose. The tools gleam in the dim light, reflecting the seriousness of the scene. He first secures the submissive in restraints, ensuring her comfort and safety are paramount. The leather cuffs are snug but not constricting, a testament to his careful attention to detail.

As the scene progresses, the Dom employs a variety of implements, each designed to elicit sensations that range from pleasure to intensity. Floggers with soft suede tails caress the submissive's skin, followed by the deliberate use of a riding crop that delivers a sharp, controlled sting. The Dom's movements are fluid and precise, ensuring that the sensations are tailored to the submissive's desires.

The scene is a captivating ballet of power and submission, where every action and reaction are choreographed with utmost precision. The trust and communication between the two individuals are evident, as they exchange knowing looks and whispered words that reinforce their connection. It's a scene that celebrates the artistry of BDSM, where the Dom's mastery is matched by the submissive's unwavering surrender. It's a powerful testament to the depth of connection that can be achieved within this intricate world.

As we watch, I can see the connection between the two individuals, the way they communicate through looks and gestures. It's a reminder that BDSM is not solely about physical acts but also about the emotional bond that underpins it. The scene unfolds with a sense of reverence and a profound understanding of consent. It is this connection and emotional bond that I hope she sees. I want her to understand that it is not all about pain and when the relationship is not just Dom and sub, but boyfriend and girlfriend or husband and wife, the connection is about trust and love.

In another room, a more intense scene is taking place. A submissive, bound and blindfolded, is on a St. Andrew's cross, her body is exposed to a Dom who wields various implements with precision and care. The submissive's reactions are a complex mix of pleasure, pain, and desire.

The Dom is skilled, and their actions are deliberate, striking a delicate balance between pushing boundaries and respecting limits. It's a scene of sensory overload, where the submissive's world narrows down to the sensations and the connection with their partner.

As we observe, I can't help but be struck by the vulnerability and bravery of the submissive, their trust in the Dom's hands. It's a scene that highlights the importance of aftercare, of tending to each other's physical and emotional well-being once the intensity of the scene has passed.

These scenes, while intense and familiar to me, offer to her a window into a world where consent, trust, and communication are paramount. They serve as a reminder that BDSM is a diverse and intricate realm, one that encompasses a wide range of experiences and dynamics.

She didn't say anything on the way back to the condo. I could tell that she was in serious thought about the things she saw tonight and the realization that this is a part of my life.

When we get inside the condo, I can't wait to ask her how she feels about me and what saw.

"Aaliyah, I need to know what you are thinking about what

you found out tonight and does knowing about this part of my life change the way you feel about me?" I ask.

"Right now, I need time to think. Time to think about what I saw, how I feel and what all of this means for us. I don't know if I can or that I am what you want and need. I need time to process this and to even think about my own sexual desires and if I am a sub and…. Just everything," she tells me and then heads to her room.

* * *

On Sunday, things are weird between us, and I try to lighten the mood. We spend the day watching TV. We barely spoke to each other, but I knew that she needed time and time I would give her. I didn't mention anything about the party, BDSM, or how she felt. We ate the leftover lasagna she cooked the day before. After lunch we packed our bags and headed to the airport to head back to Ouray.

I know that Aaliyah witnessed several scenes at the party last night with the people engaged in various forms of BDSM play, from light bondage to more intense experiences. I know it's an eye-opening experience for her, and I can see that it's left her with a lot to consider.

We land back in Ouray, and I drive her home. She gets out the car, I grab her bags while she unlocks the door. When she walks in, I follow her and drop her bags at the bottom of the stairs.

"Thank you again for the trip to New York. I really did have a wonderful time, all in all," she says.

"You're welcome," I tell her and lean in and kiss her on the cheek before walking out. I can't help but wonder about the future and the choices that await us.

Chapter Thirteen

Aaliyah

It's been two days since we got back home to Ouray and the revelation of Madden's hidden world in New York has left me with a whirlwind of emotions and a burning curiosity about this enigmatic side of him. As our relationship seemed to have deepened, while we were gone, right up until that party. I was so surprised and shocked at first about him being into BDSM, but the more I reflect on that night and what I saw the more I become intrigued the BDSM lifestyle and the desires I felt watching it. Desires that I don't even know where they came from and why I felt them. I have never had those desires before. Is that because I have never seen BDSM play before or because I really don't have those types of desires? I have no idea and I need some answers. It is time to ask Madden some questions.

I pick up the phone and call him. He answers on the first ring, "Aaliyah, hello."

"Madden, I need to ask you some questions. There are things I want to understand about Saturday nights party, things I want to understand about you and your desires. Will you come over at 7 pm tonight for dinner?" I ask.

"Yes, I can come have dinner with you and answer any questions that you may have," he replied.

"Okay, I will see you then," I tell him, and we both say goodbye and hang up.

In the quiet moments of the rest of the day, I find myself working through my thoughts, trying to make sense of it all. The complexities of human desires are far from straightforward, and I can't help but wonder what led Madden to explore this realm. His honesty about his past experiences and his secret desires has awakened a torrent of questions in my mind.

* * *

Madden shows up at 7 pm on the dot and as we are eating dinner, I take a deep breath and look into his eyes. "Madden, there are so many things I want to know, to understand. Can we talk about this now? I have so many questions."

He nods, his expression filled with warmth and understanding. "Of course, Aaliyah. I'm here to answer your questions. But let's finish our dinner first and we can go sit in the living room and you can ask me anything you want to know."

"Okay, I can wait until then," I tell him.

As Madden and I sat in my living room, my curiosity about the world of BDSM had reached a point where I couldn't contain my questions any longer. I looked at him, a mix of intrigue and vulnerability in my eyes, and finally, I decided to voice what had been on my mind.

"Madden," I began, taking a deep breath, "I appreciate your patience, and I want to understand more about this lifestyle. Can you tell me how you got into all of this?"

As we delve into our conversation, I begin by asking about his past and what led him to explore the world of dominance and submission. His openness in sharing his experiences and feelings allows me to understand his journey better. I listen, captivated by his stories, and slowly, my apprehensions begin to ease.

He met my gaze with a reassuring smile, and I could tell he was prepared to share his journey with me. "It all began in college," he explained. "I had a close friend who introduced me to the BDSM community. It opened my eyes to a world that was about more than just physical acts. It was about trust, communication, and exploring desires."

Listening to his words, I nodded, trying to grasp the significance of his journey. "But what does it mean for us, for our relationship?"

Madden's smile remained warm and patient. "For us, it means deepening our connection in a way that feels right for both of us. It's about exploring boundaries and desires while always prioritizing consent and trust. It can enhance our intimacy and bring us even closer."

I considered his response and then asked, "And as a Dom, what are your desires and responsibilities in this dynamic?"

Madden's expression grew earnest as he leaned in, "As a Dom, my desire is to guide and protect you, to create an environment where you can fully express your desires and trust me completely. I'll lead, but I'll also listen to your needs and boundaries. It's about understanding your pleasure and your limits."

His words eased some of my concerns, and I sought clarification, "So, it's not just about you having control over me?"

Madden shook his head. "No, not at all. It's a partnership, a symbiotic relationship. I may lead, but it's all based on your consent. We communicate openly, and your needs and feelings are just as important as mine. It's about creating a space where both of us can explore and grow."

His reassurance made me feel more at ease, and I continued, "And it's a journey, right? We can take it at our own pace?"

Madden's smile remained steady. "Exactly. There's no rush. We'll explore and discover together, adjusting our dynamic as we go. The most important thing is that we're on this journey together, with trust and open communication."

As I processed his responses, I realized that this conversation was a significant step in our exploration of the BDSM lifestyle. It was a path we were embarking on together, marked by mutual respect and a deep sense of trust, and it filled me with a growing sense of connection and understanding between us.

The night carries a blend of curiosity, understanding, and a growing sense of connection. The atmosphere in my home becomes charged with a different kind of energy, one that's been building over time. It's a blend of vulnerability and trust, the pillars on which our relationship stands.

As the evening progresses, our conversation evolves into a deeper connection. We talk about our past, the feelings we held back in high school, and the moments that passed us by. Madden's admission that he had feelings for me in those years leaves me with a sense of nostalgia. I never realized how he perceived me back then, and the revelation brings a newfound warmth to our connection.

It was in that moment that I want to pick up where we left off on his couch in New York. I want him so badly. I want to show him how I feel about him, how deep those feelings are. I get up off the couch, stand in front of him and hold out my hand for him to take it. He looks up at me with a little confusion in his eyes. I shake my hand and my head at him. He takes my hand and I lead him upstairs to my bedroom.

We walk in and I let go of his hand and undress as he watches me. When I am completely naked, I kneel before him like I saw the subs do at the party on New Year's Eve. He just stands there for a minute before he undresses. With the last of his clothes thrown on the floor, he walks over to me and puts his hand out.

"Tonight it is about our love for each other and just that one small act of submission means more to me than you know. Tomorrow we can start training you to be my sub, tonight, I just want to pleasure my girlfriend," he says.

I take his hand and he leads me to the bed. We make love, not as a means to explore his hidden desires but as a testament to the bond that's grown between us.

As we lie entwined, the air filled with the warmth of our shared connection, Madden speaks softly, his voice laced with emotion. "Aaliyah, I want you to know that what I feel for you now is deeper than anything I ever felt in high school. I was always afraid to approach you back then, but today, I know that my heart belongs with you."

"Mine are stronger for you now too and I want to try and fulfill your desires. In that process, I want to find answers to the desires that I felt that night at the party," I tell him.

We kiss and fall asleep in each other's arms. I never felt happier or at peace than I did laying in his arms.

* * *

Madden

The night spent with Aaliyah in her warm embrace has left me with a sense of contentment and longing. Our relationship has taken a passionate turn, and the air around us is charged with a newfound intensity. As I wake up the next morning, sunlight streaming through her bedroom window, I find myself gazing at her sleeping form with affection and desire.

Her eyes flutter open, and her smile is the first thing I see. It's a sight that fills my heart with warmth, knowing that we share something special. Aaliyah's soft morning greetings are a melody to my ears, and as we cuddle together under the cozy sheets, the world outside seems to fade away.

We talk about the moments we've shared; about the connection we've found in each other's arms. It's a time of vulnerability, as we lay bare our feelings. She expresses her concern about not being the woman I need, her uncertainty about joining me in the lifestyle I've been a part of.

I listen attentively, my fingers gently tracing patterns on her skin. "Aaliyah, I understand your concerns, and I respect your need for more time to think about it. This is an important decision, and it's not something that should be rushed."

Her eyes search mine for understanding, and I continue. "If you'll give me a chance, Aaliyah, I can show you things slowly. It's not about pushing you into something you're not comfortable with; it's about us discovering what works for both of us."

Aaliyah nods, her expression reflecting the gratitude she feels. The morning unfolds with affection and a renewed understanding between us. The depth of our connection grows, and as we lie entwined, I know that we can get through this test

Chapter Thirteen

and on the other side we will be stronger for it.

Chapter Fourteen

Aaliyah

It has been three days since our conversation about Madden's hidden desires and our night of love making. The conversation left me in a state of contemplation. It's clear that Madden's world of dominance and submission is a complex one, filled with nuances and rules that I don't understand yet, but I need and want to understand them. While I'm not sure if I'm ready to fully embrace this lifestyle, I've decided to let Madden show me what it entails, to better understand the principles and dynamics. I sincerely want to try this for him.

It is a Friday night and Madden is going to spend the weekend with me and teach me about BDSM. He is so patient and understanding, knowing that this is uncharted territory for me. He is taking his time introducing me to the world of dominance and submission. He is giving me the space to ask questions and explore at my own pace. I've come to realize that it's not solely about one person dominating another but rather a consensual exchange of power and trust.

He's explaining the importance of clear communication and boundaries, the foundation upon which this world stands. As we explore this new territory together, he emphasizes that every act is based on trust and consent. It's not about forcing or pressuring, but rather about understanding desires and limits.

"Okay babe, let me break down a few things for you. Let's start your lesson for the day. BDSM is a multifaceted realm of erotic and psychological play that can include various activities. Here's a more detailed breakdown: Bondage: This involves restraining a partner using ropes, cuffs, or other restraints. It's about the power dynamic and the thrill of being in control or surrendering that control. Discipline: Discipline in BDSM refers to consensual punishment and rewards. It often includes spanking, flogging, or other forms of impact play. Dominance and submission: At the core of BDSM are power dynamics. One partner, the Dom, takes control, while the other, the Submissive, willingly surrenders control. This can involve role-playing and following agreed-upon rules. Sadism and Masochism: Sadism is derived from the pleasure of inflicting pain or humiliation, while masochism is the enjoyment of receiving it. It's important to note that in BDSM, all activities are consensual," he explains.

I listen as he continues.

"Now I am going to breakdown bondage even further. Bondage is a fundamental component of BDSM that involves restraining a partner, often using ropes, cuffs, or other restraints. It plays a significant role in the exploration of power dynamics, trust, and intimacy within the BDSM lifestyle. At its core, bondage is about power and control. It allows one partner to exert authority over the other, creating a power exchange dynamic. The person applying the restraints is typically referred to as the Dom, while the one being bound is the Submissive.

The foundation of all BDSM activities is consent and trust. Before engaging in bondage, explicit consent and boundaries are established through open communication. It's crucial for all parties involved to feel safe and secure throughout the experience. There are various forms of bondage, each with its unique characteristics: Rope Bondage: Shibari, a Japanese art form, involves intricate rope patterns that can be both visually stunning and highly restraining. Restraints: Cuffs, straps, and other restraints provide a secure and controlled means of binding a partner. Duct Tape and Bondage Tape: These can be used to create quick and efficient restraints, but care must be taken to avoid injury. Predicament Bondage: Involves restraining a person in such a way that they have to maintain a specific position or face uncomfortable consequences if they move. Safety Precautions: Safety is paramount in bondage. Rigorous attention must be paid to circulation, breathing, and any signs of discomfort. It's essential to have safety shears on hand to quickly release restraints if necessary. Bondage Artistry: For many in the BDSM community, bondage is an art form. Shibari, for example, involves intricate knot-work and patterns that are both visually appealing and functional. The aesthetics of bondage can be as important as the sensation. Psychological Impact: Bondage often carries a strong psychological element. It can evoke feelings of vulnerability, surrender, or dominance, depending on one's role. The mental aspect of BDSM is as important as the physical. Release and Aftercare: After a bondage session, it's crucial to provide aftercare. This includes reassurance, emotional support, and physical care to ensure that all parties feel safe and cared for. Exploration and Limits: Bondage, like all BDSM activities, is a means of exploring one's desires and boundaries. It's important to continually communicate with your partner and be aware of their physical and emotional state. Community and Education: Many BDSM practitioners join local communities or online forums to learn and share experiences. These communities can provide valuable education, support, and opportunities to meet like-minded individuals," he explains.

He went on to breakdown discipline, dominance and submission, and sadism and masochism. He also included discussions about aftercare, a concept I've come to appreciate. It's the act of caring for one another physically and emotionally after an intense scene, emphasizing the importance of tending to each other's well-being.

"How do you feel about everything we have talked about today?" he asks me.

"It is a lot, but I understand it all. Can you show me some of the positions though?" I ask.

"Of course. I can show you some pictures or there is a site with videos. What do you want to see, or do you want to see both?" he asks.

"Let's start with photos and then watch some videos," I tell him.

"Of course. Where's your laptop?" he asks.

I get up off the couch and go to the room of the dining room where I have created a little office space and grabbed my laptop. I come back and hand it to him.

He pulls up some pictures of the different bondage positions and the different toys. Then he logs into a website and we watch some videos. He also downloads a list of things for me to mark as hard limits, things I would do and things I am curious about. He asks me to go print it off and we can go through it together, that way if I have questions about any of them, I can ask him.

I did and the first thing I did was I went through the entire five-page list and mark things that I would do. Then I went through and mark the things that I knew I wouldn't do and last the things I was curious about. I left blank anything that I didn't understand. Those things we went through one by one, and he described them for me and if I still didn't quite understand them, he showed me pictures or videos.

* * *

After we spent hours of going through all of that information, we order in Italian food and sit in front of the TV to eat and watch a movie. He said that he thought we should watch the Fifty Shades of Gray series.

It is about 8 pm and the first movie comes to an end, and I am in wow mode.

"Are you tired?" I ask him.

"Not yet, you?" he asks.

"Not yet. Can we watch the second one now?" I ask.

"Of course," he replies and starts the second movie.

Three hours later and the second movie is over, and we are going to head up to shower and go to bed. I feel like I have a calmer understanding after watching the movie, even though I know it is Hollywood's best replica that they can put on the big screen.

I go into the bathroom and start the shower while Madden is cleaning up the takeout and cutting off all the lights. I step into the shower and the water feels so good as it beats against my skin and flows down my body. I see the sliding door to the shower start to move towards the front of the shower. Oh my god! *He is getting in the shower with me!*

He steps in and gets right behind me so that our bodies are touching. He leans down and starts kissing my neck and rubbing my breasts with his hands, taking my nipples between his fingers rubbing them and then giving them a slight pinch. I stand there, still, letting out little moans from deep in my throat that I have no control over.

He turns us around so that the water is on his back and my back is against the wall. He picks me up and slides me down on his massive manhood. He makes love to me in the shower. He is sliding me up and down on his dick, going faster and harder as time goes. I feel so full and alive as an orgasm takes over and it just keeps going. Oh my, this is the longest orgasm I have ever had.

When we came together, he turned me back around so the water can hit me, and he washed me. I got out and he washed himself. We get in the bed, and I am exhausted, but I lay there reflecting on the events of the day. I lay there thinking about this world of dominance and submission and how I am coming to understand that it's not just about physical acts but also about the emotional connection that underpins it. Trust, respect, and communication are key, and I've been given the time and space to process these new revelations.

Today I have allowed Madden to show me the various aspects of this world, even if I'm not yet participating in the practices. I watch, I listen, and I ask questions, taking in the intricate web of sensations, desires, and boundaries that make up this lifestyle. I can see already how me exploring this world that he is a part of has deepening our connection in a way I haven't anticipated. I'm still uncertain about the extent to which I will embrace this lifestyle. I am coming to appreciate the passion, trust, and intimacy that underpin it. I'm reminded, however, that love knows no boundaries, and it's the bond we share that makes our relationship unique and exhilarating.

Chapter Fifteen

Aaliyah

Even after the weekend we spent with him teaching me about the BDSM lifestyle the path I'm treading with him is still one of uncharted territory. The introduction to his world of dominance and submission has opened up a realm I never thought I'd explore. It is filled with complexities, introspection, and moments of hesitation.

My days are consumed with thoughts, contemplation's, and a constant struggle to make sense of it all. This world he's introducing me to is intricate and layered, filled with rules, desires, and a profound sense of trust. As I try to understand its intricacies, I find myself at a crossroads, grappling with my feelings and convictions. The dilemma that plagues me is multifaceted. On one hand, there's my deep affection for Madden, a love that's grown in strength and intensity. I can see the sincerity in his eyes, the passion with which he reveals this hidden aspect of his desires. There's a part of me that yearns to connect with him on this level, to embrace this new facet of our relationship. Yet, on the other hand, I'm filled with apprehension and doubt. The world of dominance and submission is so far removed from the life I've known. The power dynamics, the sensations, the intensity, it's all so overwhelming. I grapple with my own reservations, questioning if I have the strength, the courage, and the desire to fully immerse myself in this world.

I lie awake at night, contemplating the future, wondering if I can find a way to bridge the gap between my love for him and my uncertainty about this world, he's introduced me to. It's a tumultuous storm of emotions, one that has me caught between the fierce desire to embrace his passions and the cautious reluctance that stems from my own insecurities. In his patience and understanding, he stands beside me through it all. He recognizes the turmoil within me and offers support and guidance. His reassurance is a balm to my wavering heart, but the dilemma remains, a complex puzzle I'm still trying to solve.

As I sat in my living room, I am having myriad of thoughts and concerns within me. It was a world I had never ventured into, and my mind was racing with questions and uncertainties. I keep asking him questions and seeking clarity. I am surprised that he has not gotten tired of me asking so many questions. I feel like I keep repeating the same ones.

I think about my concerns, first and foremost, I am anxious about my own understanding and acceptance of this lifestyle. I have always considered myself open-minded, but the idea of surrendering control, even in a consensual manner, felt like uncharted territory. The fear of the unknown lingered in my thoughts. I worry about how it might impact our relationship. We had a connection that felt profound and real, but would introducing this new dynamic change everything? Would we lose the simplicity and comfort of our existing bond? It is a risk I am willing to take, but not without reservations.

Additionally, I grappled with the idea of societal judgment. BDSM was a realm often shrouded in misconceptions and misconstrued as something deviant. I am concerned about the perception of others, fearing potential misunderstandings and prejudice. How will we navigate a world that is sometimes misunderstood or unfairly stigmatized?

The more Madden shares his insights, the more my concerns deepened. The introduction of toys and various elements like nipple clamps and anal plugs, while intriguing, also bring a sense of trepidation. The prospect of pain and pleasure intricately intertwined challenge my preconceived notions of comfort and boundaries. Most significantly, I question my own desires and limits. How far am I willing to explore this new aspect of our relationship? Can I truly embrace the principles of dominance and submission? Do I possess the resilience to navigate the intensity of the emotions and experiences that awaited us?

Despite these concerns, there was one undeniable truth, my growing feelings for Madden. His patience, understanding, and the genuine connection we share make me willing to explore this world with him. It is a leap of faith into the unknown, but is it one that I am willing to embark upon? With every question that arose, I knew that we would navigate this path together, with trust, understanding, and love as our guiding lights, but was it something that I really wanted to be a part of. I need to make sure that I am doing this because I want it and not to just simply, please Madden.

As I think about my concerns, I also have to notice the

intriguing aspects that stir my curiosity and, in some cases, ignite my desires. These discoveries are transforming my perspective, pulling me closer into making the decision to join him in the lifestyle.

One of the first things that intrigues me is the element of trust. Trust was the cornerstone of this lifestyle, and witnessing the profound trust between the Dom and the sub was awe-inspiring. It fascinates me how two individuals can rely on each other to navigate the intricacies of pleasure, pain, and vulnerability. It is a different form of intimacy, one built on a foundation of absolute trust, and I can't help but admire it.

The power dynamics are equally captivating. The exchange of control and submission is not about force but about consent and communication. It is a mutual agreement to explore the boundaries of one's desires. The way Madden explained these dynamics, emphasizing that the submissive held an unspoken power, is intriguing. It shows me that this world isn't just about the Dom's control but also about the submissive's choice to surrender.

The exploration of sensations is another aspect that fascinates me. It isn't solely about pain; it was about the blend of pleasure and pain, the way they intertwined, creating an array of emotions and sensations. The introduction to various toys and tools, like nipple clamps and anal plugs, allowed for a broad spectrum of experiences, each tailored to individual preferences. It was the idea of discovering what brought pleasure and arousal in the midst of sensation play that intrigued me. Even though I am not to thrilled about the idea of nipple clamps or anal plugs yet.

Communication and negotiation are key components of this lifestyle. The meticulous planning and open conversations between partners ensure that boundaries are respected, desires are understood, and consent is paramount. The level of communication and honesty requires piqued my interest. It makes me appreciate the care and consideration that go into each encounter. The exploration of fantasies and desires is also a powerful element. It is about embracing one's innermost fantasies and bringing them to life within the bounds of consent and trust. The idea that we can explore and fulfill our deepest desires without judgment or shame was liberating. It awakens a sense of freedom to express our desires authentically.

Most importantly, it was Madden's unwavering support, understanding, and patience that fuels my curiosity and desires. His commitment to guiding me at my own pace, respecting my boundaries, and allowing me to explore this world gradually is a testament to his care and affection. His desire to share this part of his life with me, not as a requirement but as an invitation, makes me feel cherished and valued.

These intriguing facets of the lifestyle were drawing me in, slowly erasing my initial reservations and doubts. While the path ahead remains uncertain, I can't deny the growing fascination and desire to explore this world with him. I know that our love is a powerful force, but my apprehension persists. The tension between my desire to connect with Madden on this new level and my doubts about my own ability to do so is a constant struggle. It's a dilemma that haunts my thoughts, keeps me awake at night, and sends my mind into a whirlwind of uncertainty.

I love him with a depth I've never known before, and I'm willing to explore new horizons for the sake of our connection. But the dilemma I face is not one that can be easily resolved. It's a journey of introspection, exploration, and understanding, one that I must navigate at my own pace, weighing the love I feel against the apprehension that lingers within me. The path ahead remains unclear, and the answers are yet to be found.

Chapter Sixteen

Madden

It has been weeks since I took Aaliyah to New York and introduced her to BDSM at the New Year's Eve play party. Sharing my desires and introducing Aaliyah to the world of dominance and submission was a decision that didn't come lightly. It wasn't just about fulfilling my own desires; it was about nurturing a connection with her that I had never experienced before. As I patiently guide her through the intricacies of this lifestyle, I can't help but reflect on the profound impact it has on our relationship.

The last few weeks Aaliyah's gradual immersion into the lifestyle is an exploration of trust, consent, and mutual understanding. The principles and dynamics that govern this world are complex, but I am committed to teaching her with patience and care. Explaining the importance of communication, negotiation, and boundaries is a fundamental part of our journey.

I share with her the significance of trust as the cornerstone of any BDSM relationship. It was the element that allowed us to surrender to vulnerability, knowing that we were in safe hands. The depth of trust between us was awe-inspiring, and as I watched her understanding of it grow, I couldn't help but feel a profound sense of connection. The dynamics of power exchange fascinated me, and it was essential for Aaliyah to grasp that submission isn't about weakness but about a choice, a consensual surrender. The way she embraced this concept, realizing that it was about her own power was a revelation. It showed me her strength and independence.

Sensation play was an exploration of desire and pleasure, and I carefully showed her various toys and tools. I emphasized that this world is about discovering what brought us pleasure, even in the midst of intensity. Her curiosity and willingness to explore the boundaries of her desires were inspiring.

Communication and negotiation were central to our journey, and I taught her that every encounter requires open and honest conversations. The way she navigated these discussions, expressing her boundaries and desires, showed me her commitment to this world and to our relationship.

The freedom to explore our fantasies and desires without judgment or shame was a powerful element of this lifestyle. It allowed us to connect on a deeper level, embracing our innermost desires and bringing them to life. Aaliyah's growing comfort in sharing her fantasies with me was a testament to the trust and understanding we had cultivated.

I couldn't help but feel an overwhelming sense of affection and admiration for Aaliyah. Her openness, her willingness to learn and embrace this world, and her patience in exploring it at her own pace touched my heart. I believe that her joining me in this lifestyle will only strengthen our relationship.

Her presence in this world is not a requirement but an invitation, a choice she made out of love and trust. I cherish every moment we share, relishing the connection we were building. The support and understanding she shows me, as well as her willingness to explore her own desires, filled me with profound affection.

As I watched her navigate this uncharted territory, I couldn't help but feel a sense of pride. Our love has grown stronger, and I knew that whatever path she chose, it would be the right one for us. The bond we had formed through this exploration was one that I knew would stand the test of time, fortified by trust, consent, and an unwavering love for each other.

Chapter Seventeen

Aaliyah

I have reached that critical point in our relationship. It is both thrilling and nerve-wracking. The decision looming overhead is one that has the power to change the course of our journey. It is a moment of introspection, where I find myself carefully weighing the pros and cons once more. On one hand, I have witnessed the depth of connection, trust, and intimacy that this lifestyle could bring into our relationship. The sense of freedom and exploration, the heightened passion, and the profound understanding we can develop were undeniable advantages. I have grown to appreciate the importance of consent, communication, and the power dynamics at play in this world. Yet, on the other hand, there were lingering doubts and uncertainties. It was a path where the unknown came with a degree of apprehension. The range of experiences, from gentle to intense, was both exciting and intimidating. I have to question whether I am ready to embrace the lifestyle physically, to explore it further alongside Madden.

Ultimately, it is the fact that my love for Madden and the connection we share are paramount. I have fallen for the man he is, for the strength of his character and the depth of his affection. His desires were a part of him, a facet of his identity that he has revealed to me with unwavering trust. It is time for me to accept this part of him, to try and fit myself inside of this lifestyle and embrace my desires and the lifestyle as part of our relationship.

I decide to call Madden over for dinner, an intimate setting where I would share my decision. As I set the table, I can't help but feel a mix of excitement and nervousness. It is a conversation that has the potential to redefine our relationship, to take it to new heights.

When he arrives, I open the door and feel there is a noticeable sense of anticipation in the air.

"Come in Madden," I tell him as I open the door further to let him inside.

"Hey beautiful," he says as he comes inside and stops in front of me and gives me the sweetest kiss on my lips. I can't help but smile.

I close the door and he says, "Wow, it smells good. What did you cook?"

"It is London Broil with Rosemary and Thyme, mash potatoes, asparagus and homemade yeast rolls," I tell him.

"I cannot wait to dig in!" he said as we walked into the dining room where I had already set the table.

We sit down and enjoy the meal sharing affectionate glances and unspoken sentiments. We engage in small talk. Once we were finished eating, we clear our plates and put way the dishes. We walk into the living room with our glasses of wine and sit down on the couch.

Sitting on there on the couch in my living room, I know I have to share my decision with Madden. We have spent numerous days exploring the world of BDSM, and now it was time for me to tell him that I have made my decision.

I turn to him, meeting his gaze with a firm resolve. "Madden," I began, my voice steady but tinged with emotion, "I've made my decision."

He nods, his eyes are full of curiosity and support, "Go on, Aaliyah. I'm here to listen."

My heart raced as I continued, "I want to try it, Madden. I want to fully participate in this lifestyle, to explore my desires as well as yours."

His gaze never wavers from mine, and his eyes seem to reflect a range of emotions. "Aaliyah," he said, "I'm honored that you've chosen to embrace this journey with me. Your willingness means the world to me."

His hand finds mine, and he gently squeezes it, reassurance in his touch. "I'll be your guide, Babe, to ensure your safety and fulfillment in this exploration for you. Your trust is a precious gift."

I can't help but smile, the excitement and anticipation bubbling inside me. "I want to learn and grow alongside you, Honey. I trust you, and I'm ready for us to explore our desires together."

He leans in, and our lips meet in a tender kiss, a silent affirmation of our shared path. "I promise to cherish your trust, Babe, and guide you with care and respect."

The bond between us deepens as we discuss our desires and boundaries, laying the foundation for my joining him into the world of BDSM. My decision to actively engage in this world marks a significant moment in our relationship, one filled with promise and growth. I was ready for the adventure, to learn, to experience, and to explore this lifestyle with him by my side. The decision marks the beginning that will test our trust, vulnerability, and mutual understanding. We are embarking on this path together, one that holds the promise of deep connection and shared exploration.

I stand up from the couch now and lead him to the bedroom where we have shared countless moments of intimacy but had not yet stepped into the lines of BDSM. There were unspoken words of agreement as to what type of intimacy we were going to have tonight.

When we got into the bedroom, he shut the door and leans against it. He looks at me and says, "Get your wand and two scarfs. Lay them on the nightstand. Undress and be laying on the middle of the bed when I return." He opens the door and walks out again.

I grab the items he requested, undressed and got in the middle of the bed.

He comes back in with a glass of ice and a feather. No idea where he found that at. He walks up to the bed and as he blindfolded me with one of the scarfs, I felt a surge of vulnerability and excitement. My senses heightened, every touch and sound magnified. The other silk scarf that bound my wrists to the bedpost was a symbol of consent, a silent agreement that I trust him implicitly.

The sensations began with the soft caress of a feather, tracing patterns across my skin. It was gentle and tender, a prelude to the pleasures to come. The contrast of ice against the warmth of my flesh sent shivers down my spine, a testament to the power of sensation play.

Madden's hand came into play, delivering controlled, rhythmic spanks across my thighs and stomach that stirred a delightful mix of sensations, from a pleasurable sting to an electrifying thrill. It was an embodiment of our connection, a dance between power and submission.

"Spread your legs and lift up your knees," he tells me.

"Yes, Sir," I say as I do as he requested.

I hear the wand before I ever feel it. It is a powerful tool. It sends waves of pleasure coursing through me, intensifying with each passing moment. It was a reminder of the intimate exploration that lay ahead.

As I lay there, blindfolded and bound, the anticipation in the room was almost palpable. My heart raced, and I could feel the warmth of the room enveloping me. I had made my decision, and now, I was eager to fully embrace this new facet of our relationship, to explore it with Madden as my guide, my partner, and my love.

Madden's hands were gentle as he began to explore my body, his fingers tracing paths of pleasure and igniting sensations I had never experienced before. The blindfold heightened my other senses, making every touch, every breath, and every whisper of his voice even more intense. It was a thrilling, intoxicating feeling, one that I couldn't wait to delve deeper into.

His voice, a soothing yet commanding presence, guided me through this intimate exploration. "Trust, Aaliyah," he whispered, his breath warm against my ear. "Trust in us and in our connection."

With every word, I felt a growing sense of trust in Madden, a trust that extended far beyond the physical. It was trust in our love, our bond, and our mutual desire to explore this world together. The journey we had embarked on was uncharted territory, but I felt an unwavering sense of security in knowing that we were navigating it together.

The sensations he elicited from my body were a revelation. The pleasure, the intensity, and the vulnerability combined to create an experience unlike any other. The bonds that held me were both physical and emotional, a reflection of our deepening connection and shared exploration.

I surrendered to his touch, allowing myself to fully embrace the experience. My body responded eagerly, my desires laid bare, and my trust unwavering. The blindfold prevented me from anticipating his every move, adding an element of surprise that kept me on the edge of anticipation.

Madden continued to guide me, alternating between caresses, kisses, and gentle strokes. His words were a soothing presence, reassuring me that I was in safe hands. With each moment, I felt a deeper connection to him, an intimacy that transcended the physical.

In this moment, I was more than willing to let go of my inhibitions, to explore the depths of my desires with him by my side. We were venturing into uncharted territory, discovering new aspects of ourselves and our relationship. It was a thrilling journey, one that held the promise of growth, intimacy, and unbridled passion.

As the evening continued, our exploration deepened, and I couldn't help but revel in the connection we shared. I had made my decision, and I was ready to embrace this world with open arms.

Chapter Eighteen

Madden

I tell Aaliyah that I want to take her back to New York for her to experience the lifestyle with other people who not only participate but live the lifestyle. She agreed.

As we arrived back in New York, I could sense a mixture of excitement and nervousness in Aaliyah's demeanor. This was a significant step in our relationship, and I was both eager and anxious to show her more of my world, starting with the playroom in my condo.

We go inside of the condo, and I drop our luggage in my bedroom. I grab hold of her hand and take her through my bedroom to a door that was made to look like another closet. I open the door and behind it is another soundproof door with a keypad. After unlocking the door with the code, I held it open for her, and she steps inside. Her eyes widen as she took in the room, which was filled with various BDSM equipment, from restraints to floggers and other toys that adorned the space. The room is dimly lit, with the soft glow of candles casting flickering shadows on the walls. The rich scent of leather and polished wood fills the air. Aaliyah takes in the sight, her gaze moving from the St. Andrew's Cross in the corner to the various restraints and implements neatly arranged on a table. It's a room of possibilities, where we can explore our desires and deepen our connection. It was a well-equipped space where I have experienced countless moments of pleasure and exploration and filled with possibilities, a place where we would explore new facets of our relationship.

I watched as Aaliyah's curiosity mixed with a hint of apprehension in her gaze. This was a world she was just beginning to understand, and I knew I had to guide her gently. I explain the purpose of the room, highlighting the importance of consent and communication in our play. I emphasize that her comfort and safety were my top priorities.

With her understanding, I instruct her to undress and get into the submission position, which she now knows means to kneel at the door. As she starts to follow my directions, as I left the room to prepare, I felt a wave of desire and affection for this incredible woman who has chosen to explore this aspect of life with me.

When I return to the playroom, I find her naked and kneeling before the door, her posture reflecting a mixture of trust and anticipation. I can't help but smile at her dedication and willingness to embrace something new. Her submission is a beautiful gift, and I intend to cherish it.

"Good girl," I say. "From now on, when we enter any BDSM-related space or scene, you are to address me as 'Lord.'" It is a symbolic way of acknowledging the power dynamic we are engaging in, and it is essential for our shared experiences. I admire her beauty and the trust she's placed in me as we embark on this journey together.

I guide her to the center of the room, and she stands there, her breath slightly shaky. I step closer, my hand gentle as I cup her face. "Are you sure you want to do this?" I ask, ensuring her consent and comfort are paramount.

Her eyes meet mine, and she nods. "Yes, Madden. I trust you."

I smile, appreciating her trust and willingness. "Remember, Aaliyah, your safe word is 'vanilla.' If you ever feel uncomfortable or want to stop, use it without hesitation."

With her reassurance, I tell her to stand, then I step back. Once she stands before me, completely exposed, and begin the journey of exploration. I trail my fingers down her spine, eliciting a shiver of anticipation. I slowly touch her skin is soft and warm under my touch, and I take my time to appreciate every inch of her.

I guide her to a padded leather bench and have her lie down. Her hands find the restraints, and she secures them willingly, a silent invitation for me to take control. I secure her wrists and ankles, ensuring her comfort and safety are paramount.

As I move around the room, I select a silk blindfold. I want to enhance her senses, to allow her to fully immerse herself in the experience. I tie it gently over her eyes, blocking out the visual world and leaving her with only her thoughts and sensations. With the blindfold securely in place, I use a silk scarf to gently cover her ears. Her world is now reduced to touch and sensation, heightening her awareness of every caress and impact. As I guide her into this sensory experience, I remain attuned to her responses, ensuring that she is comfortable and engaged.

I then move on to a leather paddle, its smooth surface a

contrast to the feather. I tap it lightly against her skin, gauging her reaction. Aaliyah gasps, her body tensing. I ensure each strike is delivered with precision and care, increasing the intensity gradually. Her moans and whimpers are music to my ears, a testament to the trust we share and the connection we've built. I switch between the paddle and my hand, delivering a combination of sensations. Her skin turns a delicate shade of pink as the intensity grows, and I cherish the way she embraces it.

As Aaliyah lies bound and blindfolded on the padded leather bench, I continue our exploration with a sense of reverence. Her willingness to surrender herself to me is both arousing and humbling, and I'm determined to ensure her pleasure and safety throughout our time together.

I move around the room, selecting a soft suede flogger. It's a gentle choice to begin with, one that will allow her to feel the rhythm and anticipation of impact play. I let the suede strands brush against her skin lightly, the sensation akin to a lover's gentle touch. Her body arches, yearning for more, and I oblige by increasing the intensity of the strokes. Each strike of the flogger is a dance of pleasure and sensation, and I savor the way Aaliyah's body responds. Her moans and gasps tell me that she's fully immersed in the experience, embracing both the pleasure and the sweet sting of the suede. I use my hand now the warmth of her skin under my fingertips is a testament to her arousal.

As we continue our exploration, I introduce a feather tickler to her body. The delicate touch contrasts the sensations of the flogger and my hand, providing a soothing, sensual experience. I let the feather glide along her skin, igniting shivers of pleasure and anticipation. I trace it along her skin, teasing her senses with its delicate touch. Her breath quickens as she reacts to the subtle stimulation. I let the feather dance over her body, from the nape of her neck down to her toes, reveling in her responses.

With the sensory journey well underway, I add a vibrator to our play. I tease her with the powerful device, placing it against her most intimate areas. Her body responds with quivering pleasure, and I take her to the brink of ecstasy. I sense her nearing the edge, and as she moans in delight, I make the decision to allow her release.

Once she finished, I unhook her from the restraints on leather padded bench, my touch gentle and reassuring. As she stands, I pick her up and take her over to the bed.

"Get up on the bed doggy style. Lay your arms flat out in front of you and your chest flat to the bed," I tell her.

"Yes, Lord," she replies.

I undress and get behind her and thrust into her in one powerful thrust. I hold nothing back. She starts to lift her chest and I hold her down with my hand to her back. I continue to pound into her over and over again, fast and hard making sure that she is taking every inch of me. She explodes squirting all over the bed, soaking it, but I don't stop. I can't stop. She has turned me on so much today with her submission. For at least the next forty-five minutes I continue to go hard until we both explode simultaneously.

I pull out and flip her to her back. I remove the blindfold and ear covering, and her eyes meet mine, filled with gratitude and satisfaction. Her trust and the intensity of our experience have deepened our connection, and I feel a sense of fulfillment in the trust she has placed in me.

We take a moment to savor the aftermath of our play, our breathing gradually returning to normal. I climb up on the bed and pull her to me. As she lies beside me, I pull her close, and we share a tender embrace.

"I'm here to guide you," I say softly, brushing a strand of hair from her face. "Your desires are important to me, and I'm committed to exploring this world together, at your pace."

She looks into my eyes, a mix of contentment and desire in her gaze. "Thank you, Madden. I trust you, and I'm ready to continue this journey with you."

In that moment, as our bodies entwine and our connection deepens, I know that our exploration of desires and pleasure has only just begun. Her submission is a gift, a testament to her trust, and I am determined to cherish it, to nurture it, and to deepen our bond. As I continue to guide her through this journey of exploration and desire, I know that we are building something extraordinary together.

About the Author

She is from a small coastal town in North Carolina and currently resides in Florida. She started reading romance novels, watching soap operas and romance/drama movies with her mother as a teenager. She then started enjoying horror, mystery, and thrillers. Her imagination and creativity started her to write her own romance novels.

Ireland started writing contemporary romance and contemporary with a little erotica and spread her wings into dark romance, reverse harem and paranormal romance.

You can connect with me on:
- https://linktr.ee/irelandlorelei
- https://linktr.ee/irelandlorelei
- https://linktr.ee/irelandlorelei

Subscribe to my newsletter:
- https://linktr.ee/irelandlorelei

Also by Ireland Lorelei

She has written the following Series:
Seals and Bounty (7 Books) - Dark Romance
Second Chance (5 Books) - Contemporary with Erotica
Vegas Blue written in Susan Stokers World (4 Books) - Contemporary
The Powerful & Kinky Society - Dark Billionaire Romance Series - Ongoing

She has written the following Standalone's:
Anonymous Love - Contemporary
Don't Tap Out (Part 1) & Don't Tap Out Again (Part 2) - Dark Romance
Entangled (Part 1) & UnEntangled (Part 2) - Contemporary with Erotica
From the Ashes - Dark Romance
Island Christmas - Contemporary
Just Breathe - Dark Romance
Naughty or Nice - Cuffs, Clamps & Candle Wax - Dark Romance
Netflix & Chill - Contemporary
Secret Spark - Dark Romance
Waves of Emotions - Contemporary with Erotica
Yes Please - Dark Romance

She has written in Anthologies:

Friends to Lovers; Mistletoe Kisses; Lovely Benefits; Personal Demons; Falling For My Best Friend, My Boyfriend's A Stripper, Vegabond Series

She published a collection of her short stories in "Dreams Come True". and she released her first "Authors Planner" in 2022.

Masquerade Party - The Powerful & Kinky Society Series Book One

Michael Anderson is the young billionaire bachelor who is the owner and CEO of *The Royal Grande Hotels and Resorts* and she's a new entry level marketing assistant in his marketing department. He's walked by her a hundred times in his offices and never really noticed her.

Abigail Baker is an average just out of college, entry level marketing associate at one of the biggest hotel and resort chains in the world. Her career goals are to work her way up the marketing chains to Chief Marketing Officer. She is focused and keeps her personal life and work life separate.

Abigail meets a man at a masquerade party and unbeknown to her at the time, he is the owner and CEO of the company that she works for. For the next several encounters at similar parties, she never recognized him as her CEO and of course he didn't even know she existed on his payroll. By the time she realizes who he is, they have already began to play.

He brings out her deepest sexual desires. She wants to learn more about the BDSM world and offers to teach her how to be a sub, but not just any sub, his sub.

What happens when this well established man who is fifteen years older than her, awakens sexual desires that she never knew she had? Can they both keep their personal life and business separate? Can they keep their growing feelings for each other at bay and stick to the contract?

Back Where It Began - The Second Chance Series Book One

Two people, two high school crushes, who never knew how the other felt and yet somehow fate had put them together years after graduation.

Sylvia Taylor had fallen madly in love with her old high school classmate. What had started as a high school crush turned into just two old friends hanging out with getting to know each other better and catching up, turned into months of seeing each other regularly. She never anticipated she would fall in love with him. Not after her last relationship had left her with walls up and heart guarded. It felt like as soon as she let the walls come down, it would all shatter around her. It was a Saturday morning in February when the dream romance came to a crashing end.

Wes Hamilton had the biggest crush on Sylvia Taylor in high school. So, when she reached out to him about his motorcycle, he jumped at the chance to get to know her now and spend time with her. He never imagined that he would fall in love with her. His past marriage had put such a bad taste in his mouth that he swore off relationships. In the end, it would be that bad taste and fear of it failing, which caused him to never tell her how he felt. So, he ended up doing the one thing he said he never wanted to do, hurt her.

Five months after their breakup that had left her devastated, she had no choice but to make that phone call that would change their lives forever. She never expected what happened next.

Milton Keynes UK
Ingram Content Group UK Ltd.
UKHW012248291123
433483UK00001B/22